MISTRESS OF INSIGHT

AMANDA LABONTÉ

Published in Canada by Engen Books, St. John's, NL.

Library and Archives Canada Cataloguing in Publication

Title: Mistress of insight / Amanda Labonté.
Names: Labonté, Amanda, author.
Description: Series statement: Daughters of aether ; book 2
Identifiers: Canadiana 20210197110 | ISBN 9781774780282 (softcover)
Classification: LCC PS8623.A255 M57 2021 | DDC C813/.6—dc23

Distributed by:
Engen Books
www.engenbooks.com
submissions@engenbooks.com

First mass market paperback printing: April 2021

Cover Design: Ellen Curtis
Cover Image: DepositPhotos.com

MISTRESS OF INSIGHT

DAUGHTERS OF AETHER BOOK 2

To Margaret.
Thanks for all your amazing support.

CHAPTER ONE

The blood ran in rivulets down her arms, streaking her pristine white nightgown.

"To bed," she said, her voice growing louder as she spoke. "To bed, to bed!"

Focusing on the light of a gaslamp to keep her trance-like appearance, she wandered off stage right, not snapping back to herself until she was well within the safety of the wing.

"Oh, Miss Dumont, that was stunning," a voice whispered into the darkness. She looked up to see the outline of one of the younger actors, dressed as a simple soldier. Everyone knew better than to talk to her while she was still in character, but as she'd just finished her last scene, Adelia Dumont broke into an appreciative smile.

"Thank you," she whispered back and headed over to the backstage change area.

"I can't believe we're already at the end of our run," Celina, the costume assistant, said, setting down a fresh bowl of warm water on a table behind a screen. Adelia set her hands in it and began washing off the blood as Celina moved around, setting out a dress Adelia had worn earlier in the show. "It feels as though we've just begun."

"It does," Adelia agreed, pulling her hands out of the now pink water. Despite the fact that Lady Macbeth was hallucinating the appearance of blood, their director, Mr. Davis, had insisted on covering Adelia in a mix of syrup and carmine pigment. Apparently fake blood was all the rage in the Parisian theater and Mr. Davis wanted to up their game.

Celina handed her a clean towel and picked up the basin. "Everything is set out for your curtain call. If you need anything, holler."

Adelia changed from Lady M's bloody nightgown and back into the banquet gown from an earlier scene. She'd wear it for fifteen minutes, then change again into an evening dress.

Thinking about it, she probably spent half her time in the theater just changing outfits. Sometimes she had a team of women helping her between scenes, but she preferred moments like this, when she had the time and could just do things on her own.

As she let the blood streaked nightgown drop to the floorboards and pulled on the medieval style gown with the front fastenings, she found she was looking forward to putting Lady Macbeth to rest, at least for a little while. Playing such a tragic figure night after night took its toll.

Fastening the last button, Adelia stepped out from behind the screen to find Celina had returned to help fix her hair. Adelia's independence ran out when it came to hairstyles. She sat at a small table while Celina did a simple braid around the crown of her head.

"You must be excited about Belfast," Celina said,

twisting hair. "I wish I were going, but only the senior girls were chosen."

"I'm sure you'll get to come along next time we travel."

In truth, Adelia was both nervous and excited. The company's next job was an engagement in Belfast where they had been given special visas by the Irish government to put off a production of *The Tempest*. Adelia would get to play Miranda, one of her favorite parts. But, while no one else in the theater company knew it, that wasn't the only reason for the trip and Adelia would be playing more than one role.

As a secret agent answerable directly to the Crown, Adelia was using the rare opportunity to get on Irish soil to conduct a fact-finding mission on behalf of Britain.

But her nerves had nothing to do with the case, or with the performances. No, her anxiety was all about the agent she'd be working with. Her new *partner*.

The roar of applause from the audience cut off any further contemplation and Adelia stood up, straightening out her costume for the curtain call.

"Do I still look mad?" she asked Celina.

"Yes, but only in the best possible way."

Adelia made her way back to the wings where she was joined by Hugo St. Croix, fully decked out in his bloody Macbeth costume. She stood next to him as the rest of the cast took their bow.

"Shall we?" Hugo held out an arm to Adelia.

Though an acclaimed actor of the stage, Hugo always had a hard time masking his distaste of sharing the spotlight with the female actresses.

"I suppose you're looking forward to your run in Belfast?" Hugo asked over the applause.

Ireland had been a sore subject between them. Hugo would remain behind, preparing for a run of *Comedy of Errors*. He'd tried pretending that he didn't mind being cut from the traveling cast, especially since he was to be replaced by an up and coming Irish star. Unfortunately for all of them, Hugo wasn't that good an actor.

"It will be nice to travel," Adelia said.

Seeing their cue, Hugo led her out on stage and she curtsied under the hot lights. While in the middle of a scene she rarely noticed the gas lamps, but during curtain call she felt their heat in full force.

She wished they'd switch to aether light, but she'd been told even if they continued to sell out every night for a year the theater still wouldn't be able to afford the upgrade.

The audience was on its feet, even in the boxes and Adelia took another curtsey while Hugo bowed, not once glancing her way though she clearly heard her name being called from the floor.

Finally the curtain fell. Adelia let out a breath as Hugo released her hand. He immediately fell in with a group of young actors who made up his usual entourage. Adelia stepped away, heading for her dressing room. She passed the propmasters and set dressers who crowded the backstage. Because tonight was the last of the run, Mr. Davis, the owner of the theater, demanded that the sets be taken down right away to make way for the next production.

Adelia made it to the narrow hall where the dressing rooms were located and entered her own little oasis.

Her dressing room was large by theater standards with enough space for a dressing table, a rose-colored settee and a Chinese silk screen behind which she transformed from her stage persona back into plain old Adelia.

Millie Oliver, the senior dresser, was waiting for her and had already retrieved the other costumes Adelia had worn and had them laid out on the settee. Nearing middle age, Millie had been with the company almost from the start, but unlike so many women who worked jobs in the background, she'd never fancied herself an actress. Instead, she'd married an actor and decided that was 'more than enough to take on.'

"Good show, dear?"

"I think so," Adelia said, closing the door firmly behind her and heading for the screen. "The audience seemed appreciative."

"Indeed, they always are," Millie said, following Adelia. "Let's get you into something more appropriate. Will Captain Lancaster be by this evening?"

"He was called out to sea," Adelia said, glad her voice remained steady. She could feel a headache bloom behind her temples but as much as she wished to go home to rest, she wasn't quite finished playing her part yet.

Millie took away the medieval gown and helped Adelia into her chosen attire for the evening. The red satin felt as much like a costume as the blood soaked clothes she'd just removed.

Millie tutted as she pulled on the corset strings. "There's plenty of fish in the sea. A pretty thing like you will find a new protector in a flash."

"Of course," Adelia said, forcing a smile on her face

as she stepped out from behind the screen and took a seat at her dressing table. Millie didn't need to know that, whether she liked it or not, the position had already been filled.

Lord Fletcher hadn't bothered with the show. Instead he'd gone straight to the after party.

It wasn't as though he hadn't seen the great Adelia Dumont put on an act before and their meeting this evening would be no different.

The current soiree was being thrown by Mr. Archibald Banks, a man whose wealth was only outweighed by his terrible reputation. He'd taken over the ballroom of the London Grand to throw a party celebrating the end of the latest run of Mr. Grant Davis' theater company.

While not one of the bigger ballrooms in the city, the London Grand made up for its lack of size with its sheer opulence. Crystal chandeliers hung from a ceiling trimmed in gold. The walls were covered in a velvety blue damask and tables covered in the finest lace cloths were piled high with food and drink.

Fletcher got himself a brandy and took stock of his surroundings.

For once the gentlemen outnumbered the ladies. He noted a pair of actresses in one corner surrounded by no fewer than ten potential suitors.

Though, of course, suitor was the wrong word. These women expected an affair, not a marriage proposal.

He took in the room and was unsurprised to find that the guest of honor had yet to arrive.

Of course she was making her admirers wait.

Fletcher finished his brandy, leaving his empty glass on the tray of a passing waiter as he reached for another, just as a ruddy faced man hurried in his direction, stopping a few feet in front of him with a sweeping bow, allowing Fletcher a glimpse of the bald patch peeking through his artfully arranged hair

"My lord," Mr. Davis said as he straightened. "I did not expect you this evening."

"Did you not?" Fletcher asked.

"I had heard that you were not fond of the theater."

Apparently it was time for Fletcher to begin his own act. In addition to owning the theater company, Davis was known as the man to go to if one wanted an introduction to one of the actresses.

"The theater no. But I am a fan of the performers."

Davis turned pink with excitement. "Anyone in particular? There's a lovely up and comer with the most dazzling set of—"

"Actually, I'd like an introduction to Miss Dumont."

It took Davis the briefest moment to recover from his initial grimace. "Miss Dumont? But surely you've heard she's already ... spoken for."

"Is she?" Fletcher sipped his brandy. "I was under the impression that relationship had come to its inevitable conclusion."

Davis furrowed his brow for a moment, apparently not keen on being out of the loop. Being a former actor himself, the lapse didn't last long before Davis forced his features back into the pleasant smile he wore in the company of gentlemen.

"Perhaps you're privy to information I haven't yet been made aware of."

Fletcher sipped his drink. "Perhaps I am."

There was a stir in the room and Fletcher's gaze went to the door, though really only one woman could cause an entire ballroom to fall silent.

Still, he was unprepared for the sight that greeted him.

Miss Adelia Dumont stood in the doorway unescorted. She wore a dress of deep red that highlighted a slender hour-glass figure and set off her gold curls to perfection.

She was stunning, and of course she knew it.

With a cool smile, Adelia waltzed into the room and a hoard of gentlemen immediately descended on her, offering to fetch drinks and refreshments while she stood in the middle of her suitors, waving her fan, a half smile on her face.

Better to get the whole thing over with, Fletcher thought to himself.

"Will you excuse me?" he nodded toward Davis, not waiting for his response. He picked a champagne flute off a nearby refreshment table, setting down his mostly empty glass, and strode across the room, right into the midst of Adelia's admirers. He held the glass out to her.

"Excuse me, Miss, but you looked parched."

Though her half smile never faltered, her eyes flashed as she took in his presence. For the briefest moment, he had the impression that she was going to leave him there, holding the glass like a buffoon.

But of course she didn't.

"Thank you, my lord," she said, reaching for the glass,

her gloved fingers just barely brushing his own. "You're too kind."

"Would you care for a turn around the ballroom? I believe there's a conservatory that is quite charming."

"That would be lovely," Adelia said, never taking her eyes off him. At least her act was having the desired effect on her would-be suitors. With muttered curses they wandered off in search of other ladies to woo.

She rested her gloved hand on his offered arm, holding her champagne glass as they walked through the crowd. Neither of them spoke as they made their way through the ballroom, though they did nod at various acquaintances.

"I suppose congratulations are in order," Fletcher said, breaking the silence as they entered the conservatory and were hit with the smell of earth and greenery. It was a hexagonal room with windows on all six sides and a glass dome for the roof. Flowers and shrubs grew in boxes under the windows and a lemon tree surrounded by benches took up the center of the room. The hotel obviously hired a superior gardener to get such greenery to grow in the middle of London.

He noted it was empty of revellers and was relieved that they no longer had an audience. "I heard your latest run was without comparison."

Adelia dropped her arm and walked over to a window box, stopping in front of a yellow rose bush.

"You don't need to make conversation with me," she said, brushing her gloved fingers over the petals of one of the roses. "Surely there's no need for us to carry on an act."

Fletcher crossed his arms over his chest, watching as

she laid her still full glass on a ledge.

"As you wish. Far be it from me to force gallantry on any lady."

"Perhaps if I'd faced your gallantry at our first meeting we'd be in a different situation now," Adelia said, turning away from the roses to face him.

The conservatory felt overly warm as she rested her eyes on him.

"Are you really interested in discussing our first meeting?" Fletcher asked.

She tilted her head, her amber eyes resting on him. The color reminded him of his favorite brandy.

Which was a silly thought that he immediately pushed aside.

"No," she finally answered. "I'm not. I assume you sought me out to review the details of our assignment?"

Fletcher took a seat under the tree. He knew it was remarkably bad manners to sit in the presence of a lady who remained standing, but Adelia wasn't a lady, she was an agent.

"There isn't much to go over. The mission was already set up, I'll simply be stepping in to accompany you to Ireland instead of Captain Lancaster."

"Of course, just a simple change." Adelia put her back to him again, her focus on a Christmas cactus.

"I know you preferred Meri as your companion, however we cannot always choose our missions."

She turned to face him, her eyes no longer the color of brandy, but more like the heart of a flame.

"I've been nothing less than a model agent."

"I never said otherwise."

"And you're the last person I'll accept a lecture from on duty," she continued, drawing in a deep breath that made it hard for Fletcher to ignore the low cut of her dress.

Hard, but not impossible.

He forced his voice to remain neutral. Her show of anger actually made it easier to keep his own temper. "As I said, I'm not questioning your dedication to the cause. I merely wanted to point out that perhaps we could do our best to make the most of a difficult situation. Do you think we could look past the circumstances of our unfortunate first meeting and start over?"

"You mean the circumstances where you propositioned me to be your mistress?"

"Many women in your circumstances would have been pleased by such a request."

"You mean women of low birth? Or actresses?"

Fletcher flinched. "How often do I have to apologize for those actions?"

"Perhaps until you mean it?"

With a sigh, he stood up. He needed to do something drastic or their mutual animosity was going to throw off the entire mission. He dropped to one knee.

Adelia's eyes widened and she took a step back. "What are you doing?"

"Begging, my dear lady, for your compassion. Please forgive my extreme lapse in judgement. I was drunk."

"You were drunk," Adelia repeated.

"And stupid."

Either his words or his tone had worked to diffuse her temper. She appeared to deflate right before him.

"Do get up before someone sees you."

"You forgive me?"

"How about I agree to a fresh start?"

Fletcher got to his feet and dusted off his trousers. "That'll do for now."

Adelia took a seat on the bench Fletcher had vacated. "What's our plan?"

"I thought you'd been briefed by Meri. We're going to Ireland to see if we can find a group of young English ladies who went missing from the Cravenwood Institute."

"Yes, I know, but what's your plan for getting into Ireland? You cannot simply show up in Belfast. I have a visa through my theater company."

"You do, and your troupe will be leaving for Ireland in just under a fortnight, is that correct?"

Adelia nodded once.

"That should be just enough time for our relationship to develop so that my accompanying you on your tour won't raise eyebrows."

"You think Mr. Davis will invite you as a guest?"

"He would have let you bring Meri."

"Yes, but Meri and I have been seen together for quite some time."

Fletcher smirked. "And now you'll be seen with me."

"You think you can make it appear that we're in a relationship? In just a fortnight?"

"If necessary, I could manage in a week."

Adelia sniffed. "I'm sure you think you could."

"All we need are a few very public meetings with the right people watching. Once our alliance is established, Davis will absolutely agree to taking me along as your companion. I'm a very influential member of society."

"Yes," Adelia's tone was dry. "I had heard."

"Shall we go over potential dates? I'll be relying on your skills as an actress to convince those around us that you aren't repulsed by my attention."

"Of course, my lord," Adelia said, opening her fan and batting her eyelashes. "You needn't worry about my acting abilities."

CHAPTER TWO

Adelia stood in the middle of her mostly empty dressing room, arms out as Millie finished the alterations on her dress for Miranda's opening scene in *The Tempest*. On the floor next to them were two open trunks, one contained the clothing that she was leaving behind, while the other was being filled with the costumes she would need for her tour abroad.

"Never you worry," Millie said, taking a pin out the corner of her mouth and using it to tuck in a pleat at Adelia's waist, "I've given instructions that whoever uses your dressing room is to leave it in the same condition as they find it."

"You're so kind to always look out for me," Adelia said. And it was true. Ever since she'd come into the company four years ago at barely seventeen, Millie had taken to her like a mother duck.

There was a gentle tap at the door and Millie stepped back, taking in her handiwork before opening it. Adelia's face lit up when Lady Hazel Winchester walked in.

"Are you still free for tea?" Hazel asked, taking off her gloves and settling on the chair in front of the empty dressing table. "I know you must be quite busy getting ready for your trip."

"I don't think we'll be long," Adelia said, glancing to Millie for confirmation. "Will we?"

"I'll be all done in a minute," the dresser said. "Then you girls can be on your way."

"Is that one of your costumes for Ireland?" Hazel asked, eyeing the renaissance dress.

"It is," Adelia said, looking down at the flowing skirts in pale blue silk and velvet. "Millie has certainly outdone herself."

"She has," Hazel agreed.

"Hush now," Millie said, crouching down to stitch the hem. "I'm just the fitter."

"You're special and you know it," Adelia said. "You should have seen this costume when she started. It must not have been touched in years. Full of dust and fraying. You gave this dress a new life."

Millie didn't respond to that, but Adelia could tell by the way she straightened her shoulders that she was more than pleased with the compliment.

"All done now," Millie said, getting to her feet. "You go change and I'll make the last adjustments."

"Thanks Millie."

Millie followed Adelia behind the silk screen and un-did the buttons on the back of her costume. As Adelia slipped it off, she handed it to her dresser.

"I can get into my day dress. You can go."

"Are you sure, Miss?"

"I'm already in my corset and that's the hardest part," Adelia assured her.

Millie took the dress and headed off to make the alterations.

"I'm a little jealous of your trip to Ireland," Hazel said as the door closed behind the dresser. "It's bound to be an adventure."

"It's not as though you haven't just had an adventure yourself," Adelia said as she pulled on the deep pink skirt to her day dress. Her dress designer Madame de Meliodor had deemed pinks and reds to be her particular color.

"A simple country party is hardly the same," Hazel said.

"Again, you were hardly at a simple country party. You took down a criminal organization."

As a recent addition to their ranks, Hazel had started off on her first mission as an agent with a bang, discovering an attempt by the very proper Lady Ashburn to abduct a group of young ladies who'd been housed at the Cravenwood Institution.

With the help of her now fiance, Duncan Walters, Hazel had been pivotal in discovering the plot in time to rescue the ladies.

"I suppose, but Ireland? What an opportunity. They haven't been particularly welcoming to British visitors in recent years."

"It will be an adventure. Though I would wish to be in different company."

Adelia could hear the faint clicking of Hazel's boots as she paced the room. One thing she learned in the short time they'd been friends was that Hazel didn't stay still for too long unless her mind was engaged.

"Duncan told me you were disappointed about Meri,"

Hazel said. "I understand you two are good friends, but Lord Fletcher is great fun and he'll keep you safe. I've seen his work first-hand."

Adelia paused in the middle of buttoning her jacket. Of course Hazel had a good opinion of Lord Fletcher. She was a lady afterall. He'd always treat her with the utmost respect.

Unlike a common actress.

Adelia gave herself a mental shake. There was no point in dwelling on the negative. She was a professional after all. Both on stage and off.

"I don't suppose I could interest you in getting some lemon ices instead of tea?" Adelia asked as she stepped out from behind the screen. "I've been suffering the nagging effects of a headache and the ices always make me feel better."

"Are you sure you wouldn't rather rest?" Hazel asked. "We can go out another time."

"I can't imagine rest being a better cure than ices, can you?"

Hazel gave an enthusiastic nod. "I agree, and I could use a reprieve. I've spent the morning listening to my mother and sister argue over floral arrangements for my wedding, then when I was asked for my opinion I was scolded for having none."

"When is the blessed event?"

"Not for three months. I insisted I be given time to settle into my new role at *The Daily* before taking time off for all the wedding nonsense."

The corner of Adelia's mouth quirked. "Nonsense is it? Is that what Duncan thinks?"

Hazel tugged a stray red curl and pushed it back under her sage green bonnet. "He agrees that there's a lot of silliness in the wedding planning, but I don't think he minds the marriage part too much."

Adelia laughed. Hazel looked so sincere, she couldn't help it. "No, I don't suppose he would have proposed if the marriage part bothered him. Let's get those ices."

Fletcher sat in his usual chair in one of the drawing rooms at Burke's gentleman's club next to a well tended fireplace. He was nursing a particularly smooth French brandy but had barely registered the taste. Instead he was staring into the dancing flames trying his best not to reflect on a set of amber eyes.

"Penny for your thoughts?"

Fletcher looked up to see his friend Duncan Walters take the seat across from him. He helped himself to the brandy that rested on the small table between them.

"I assure you, it would be a poor investment on your part."

"Indeed?" Duncan's lips pulled into an easy smile. Ever since his engagement announcement, Fletcher had noticed that his usually serious friend was quick with a laugh or a grin. "Aren't you in the depths of planning the Irish mission?"

"I've already reviewed the correspondence from our undercover agents and organized a few leads."

"Do you think this will be the break we've been waiting for?"

Fletcher sipped his brandy. "I think so, assuming we can find out what happened to the other missing women—the ones who disappeared before Hazel led us to

Lady Ashburn's treason."

"If that's the case, us agents will hardly be needed going forward. At least, not until the next big case."

"Yes, I suppose so," Fletcher said, finishing his brandy in one swallow. Unlike Duncan who had a happy future filled with two loves—Hazel and his work—Fletcher found himself staring into a void.

How would he fill his time until the Agency had something to do?

But he was getting ahead of himself. They still had the mission before them to deal with.

"Hazel wished for me to pass along a message," Duncan said, leaning forward in his chair, he dropped his voice. "She thinks it's a mistake not to tell Miss Dumont about the … abilities we discovered in the ladies who were being abducted."

Fletcher frowned. "You mean the visions?"

Duncan nodded.

While on the case with Hazel, Duncan had explored the theory that the women who suffered from an affliction known as aether fever also possessed a unique psychic ability to see visions from the perspective of other people. Given that Hazel herself claimed to have the ability, and given she'd used it to help save not only herself, but about a dozen other women, Fletcher was also inclined to believe in the validity of these abilities.

It was also thanks to one of these visions that they knew to search for the missing women in Ireland, and more specifically near Belfast.

"We agreed that discretion is key," Fletcher said. "I don't want to share this information with anyone unless it's absolutely necessary."

"You don't trust Miss Dumont?"

Fletcher ran a finger around the rim of his empty glass. "I don't know her, not really."

"And yet you're going to convince all of London that you two are so involved with each other that she cannot possibly go off on tour without you?"

"That's nothing." Fletcher waved his hand. "All that I have to do is convince the gossips that Miss Adelia Dumont has favored me as her latest protector. We'll be the talk of every drawing room by this time tomorrow and I'll have an invitation to come along as a guest of the theater company within the week."

"Indeed? Surely you don't need the full week."

"I can sense the derision in your voice, but I assure you, two, possibly three outings are all that will be needed. After all, my reputation amongst the *ton* is such that they will have no trouble believing me capable of running off with an actress for a few weeks of fun."

"Perhaps after this mission it will be time to retire that reputation. It can't be comfortable for you to be perceived as a rake."

Fletcher could feel Duncan watching him. His friend was about to turn serious and that was the last thing he wanted. He swirled the brandy in his glass, watching the deep amber liquid catch the flames.

"You're mistaken, my friend. I am completely at ease in my role."

"If you say so."

Time for a change of subject.

"Tell me," Fletcher said, leaning forward in his chair, "have you been to the Bombay Spectacle? I hear it's quite something to behold."

CHAPTER THREE

"You look lovely, Miss," Lilah said as she finished sweeping Adelia's curls over her left shoulder. It was one of the maid's favorite styles and Adelia wore it often.

"I think I look a bit peaky," Adelia said, looking at her reflection with a critical eye. After parting with Hazel earlier in the day, she'd found herself on the receiving end of a raging headache. Apparently ices could not cure all.

"Should I make you another tonic?" Lilah asked, taking a step back to look Adelia over. "Or perhaps I should send a message that you are indisposed this evening?"

"No," Adelia said, rubbing her temple in a circular motion. "The tonic helped, I'll be fine to go out."

"This is your second headache in a week. Perhaps we should call Dr. Sahni?"

"No, that won't be necessary. I'm sure I just need more sleep. Now that I have a break between runs I'll catch up."

Lilah pursed her lips and let her gaze rest on the copy of *The Tempest* that was left on the corner of the dressing table. "Aren't you starting rehearsals tomorrow?"

"Just a read-through. Nothing strenuous."

Though Lilah had been her lady's maid for nearly two years, Adelia had never been completely upfront with her about her work as an undercover agent, mainly because Lilah refused to ask. The maid had to know that her mistress wasn't an ordinary actress, the simple fact that she knew that all of Adelia's supposed affairs were a ruse was evidence enough. Yet Lilah was a perfect professional.

"I'm going to make you another tonic, and a supper tray," Lilah said, pausing in the bedroom door. "You still have an hour before you need to dress. Perhaps you could rest?"

"With my hair already set?" Adelia forced a laugh. "I would never."

"You know it wouldn't take me long to fix it," Lilah muttered to herself as she walked out into the hallway, leaving Adelia alone with her thoughts. She reached out, intending to pick up *The Tempest* but her hand reached past the book and instead settled on a delicate pink box covered in enamel roses. She opened the lid, emptying the white pills inside onto the dressing table and counted them out. Twice.

Just as she'd suspected, she hadn't missed any.

A shiver ran down her spine. As soon as the headache had hit that afternoon she suspected the worst.

What if the fever was back?

Twenty-one years ago, while her mother had been out on the streets of London taking part in the King's Jubilee celebrations, the Americans had attacked. Balloons filled with poisonous aether had fallen all over the city, infecting every pregnant woman in the London area. All the women carrying male children miscarried, but the daughters survived, only to become afflicted with a sickness of the mind that resulted in headaches and uncontrolled visions that often resulted in long-term treatment in an asylum.

Adelia had been one of those affected. She'd fought her way through childhood, hiding her symptoms until she found proper treatment with Dr. Sahni. Eventually the symptoms had completely disappeared thanks to the blockers the doctor had prescribed.

The clock over her mantle chimed the half hour and Adelia gave herself a shake. She'd taken her blockers, just as she'd thought. These were just ordinary headaches and it was no wonder. Between preparing for a new part and having to work with Lord Fletcher she was under a great deal of stress.

Once this case was over, she'd be fine again.

Adelia swept the pills back into the pill box and checked her hair in her reflection before heading to her dressing room to pick out a gown for the evening.

After finishing his brandy with Duncan, Fletcher called for his steam carriage. A rusty fog clung to the early evening air, but rather than put on his mask he held his breath and hurried the few steps from the club's doorway to his waiting carriage.

The steam carriage was shaped much like a horse drawn model, though with only one small round window in the door. This was to accommodate the air filters that piped into the interior. Most hired carriages, and even many private conveyances, were painted black. It made upkeep much easier as the aether fumes in the London air often reacted with the metal causing lighter colors to turn reddish.

Fletcher's carriage was a dark blue. It still had to be painted every year, but it appeased his mother's vanity to have a carriage that didn't look like a hired hackney. His driver was dressed in the blue and gold livery that all their servants wore and even his mask had been fashioned out of blue leather with gold plated filters.

No detail was too minute to escape his mother's notice. Though, Fletcher should have been grateful that it had occurred to the great Lady Fletchingham to consider that the servants had needs at all. Some of the grander houses didn't outfit their staff with masks, leaving them to fend for themselves.

Though he'd been outdoors for mere seconds, the metallic tang from the aether mixed with the fog stuck to his tongue. On overcast days, which were more common in London than not, the aether smoke from the factories at the city's outskirts filled the air, creating a dense, reddish mist. Citizens who could afford to, wore breathing masks over their nose and mouth to filter the air. Those who couldn't afford it made do with handkerchiefs or pieces of cloth.

The steam carriage hissed to life with a jolt and began to move through the streets. It wasn't one of the latest models, but Fletcher had agreed to the interior being redone each year. His mother would have replaced this carriage three times over if she'd been given half a chance. With the majority of his peers renting carriages during the season, Fletcher wasn't about to flaunt their wealth. Besides, if his mother had her way, there wouldn't be a family fortune left to waste.

The carriage came to a stop in front of a gray stone townhome. Once again Fletcher didn't bother with a mask, instead he rushed past the iron gates and took the stairs two at a time, pausing just long enough for the dour-faced butler to open the door for him.

"Lord Fletchingham," the butler said with a stiff bow. No matter how often he'd made his wishes known, the staff refused to call him Lord Fletcher - the nickname his father had originally given him.

He assumed his mother was responsible for the formal use of his name and he could hardly blame the servants for wanting to avoid Lady Fletchingham's wrath.

"Wilson," Fletcher nodded as he headed for the stairs. His first outing with Adelia was that evening and he didn't want to be late. She hardly needed more reasons to show her disapproval.

"Your mother wishes to see you," Wilson said, forcing Fletcher to pause with one foot on the bottom step. "She awaits you in her drawing room."

Fletcher cleared his throat, forcing the easygoing attitude for which he was known to the surface.

"I'll be with her as soon as I've changed for the evening."

Wilson shuffled off to report to the lady of the house while Fletcher continued up to his rooms.

Though he'd inherited his title when he was still a teenager, Fletcher had never moved to his father's rooms. Partly because he couldn't imagine telling his mother to move—and there was no way he was setting up in the chambers next to hers—and partly because he couldn't imagine taking over a space that he so strongly associated with his father.

Which left him in the same room he'd had since he'd come home from boarding school.

"Good evening, Sir," Myles greeted him from the middle of his room where he was holding two different pairs of trousers. "Which do you wear with the navy jacket?"

"The black," Fletcher pointed at the pair on the right. "I don't suppose you had better luck getting tickets for tonight than you've had with setting out my clothes?"

"But of course." Myles dropped the trousers into a heap on the end of the bed and reached into the inside pocket of his jacket. "Box seats. And I sent the invitations, as you requested."

"Thank you." Fletcher went to the end of the bed to straighten out his clothes before the wrinkles set in. Myles had been in his employ for less than a year, though as a fellow agent, he and Fletcher had met on a case nearly two years past. Since the work of an undercover agent was somewhat inconsistent, Fletcher had offered the job as valet as means to supplement Myles' income.

It was a position he was still learning.

"I noticed that Ronnie Lovejoy was on the list of invitees for this evening."

"Yes. And?" Fletcher began unbuttoning his shirt.

"And I thought you'd finished with her company," Myles said, heading into the adjoining dressing room.

"I don't require Miss Lovejoy's company, just her proclivity to gossip."

"Of course." Myles emerged with a navy evening jacket and clean shirt, which Fletcher took from him. "You need to spread the word about Miss Dumont and she's sure to get the rumor mill going."

"There's a method to my madness," Fletcher said, fixing his cuffs.

He finished dressing and waited for Myles to give him a once over and a "you'll do" before heading off to face the inevitable.

The walk from his wing to his mother's could be accomplished in seconds, but Fletcher dragged his feet, observing the art on the walls—mainly country landscapes taken from the family estates—until he found himself at his mother's door. He knocked once and was let in by a young maid who gave a quick curtsy.

"Is that Lord Fletchingham?" His mother's voice carried into the hallway.

"Yes, my lady."

"Let him in and you're dismissed."

The maid waited for Fletcher to enter the room, then moved past, shutting the door behind her.

"You asked to see me?" Fletcher stepped into the room, coming to stand behind a pale blue sofa. His mother's room was decorated in blue, white and silver. A den befitting a snow queen.

Lady Fletchingham sat in a high backed chair, a glass of claret on the table next to her. She wore a sapphire silk dress and her dark hair, which was barely streaked with gray, was pulled back to reveal the diamonds at her ears and throat.

She looked him over, her sharp eyes settling on his cravat.

"Why do you insist on those new styles? It's so

fussy."

Fletcher forced his face to remain neutral. There was no point in allowing his mother to win points by goading him.

"I assume you didn't call me here to discuss my cravat?"

Her lips thinned for the briefest moment but she reached for her glass and her bored expression slipped back in place.

Of course, Fletcher knew it was just a mask. His mother was never anything less than calculating.

"No, the reason I called you here was to discuss your lifestyle"

"Indeed? As head of the family I was unaware I needed your approval."

"As head of the family I should have thought you needed no reminding as to your duty. You ought to be choosing a bride this season. You are very close to thirty."

"I'm not yet nine and twenty," Fletcher said, but there was little point in arguing with his mother. Given her way, she'd have had him married to a lady of her choosing years ago.

"Do I need to remind you of the promise you made to your father?"

He should have been prepared for her to bring up the vow he'd made at his father's deathbed to settle down before his thirtieth birthday, yet the reminder twisted like a knife in his gut.

"Father wanted me to be happy."

"As his only child, your father wanted you to carry on

the family name."

Fletcher could feel his emotions threatening to bubble up as they often did when he and his mother discussed his father. He fisted his hands until his knuckles turned white, grateful that the sofa hid the action from his mother's view.

"I suppose you have another list of eligible ladies for me?" He asked.

She took a delicate sip from her glass. "I've decided to try a different tactic this year. I've chosen a prospective bride for you."

Fletcher raised an eyebrow. "You've chosen for me?"

"Lady Fianna Sinclair."

Fletcher wracked his brain but couldn't remember her, though he was familiar with the Sinclair name. His father had been close with an Earl of Sinclair before his death.

"Have I met her?"

"She has only just had her come out."

"Just come out? Is she even twenty yet?"

Lady Fletchingham pursed her lips. "That is hardly an appropriate question, but I believe she is nineteen."

"That's rather young."

"A young bride will suit you quite well. Your father and I were of a similar age when we married and we were quite content."

Fletcher felt that was a slight exaggeration, but he had to agree that his parents hadn't appeared completely miserable. His earlier conversation with Duncan came back to him. The Agency's work was slowing. This could easily be his last mission for a spell. If he wanted to fulfill his promise to his father, the timing likely wouldn't get better. He could take time to settle in with his new wife, and be back to work when the next case arose.

"I'll agree to consider your choice," Fletcher said.

His mother's lips curled into a satisfied smile and Fletcher fought the immature urge to retract his offer. "I'll arrange a dinner."

"You expect me to believe you haven't already?"

His mother reached for her claret, waving him off. "I assume you have plans for the evening. I'll inform your valet once the dinner plans are finalized."

As he left his mother's drawing room, Fletcher felt a heavy feeling settling in his chest and reminded himself that he hadn't committed to anything. At least, not yet.

CHAPTER FOUR

"You have no idea where you are going this evening?" Lilah asked as Adelia adjusted the long black velvet cape around her skirts. She and her maid were waiting in the drawing room for the arrival of Lord Fletcher's carriage.

"No, but I imagine it will be somewhere very public."

There was a knock on the drawing room door and Richard, her manservant, poked his head in.

"His lordship is here."

"Did he come to the door himself?" Lilah asked, stretching her neck to look past Richard's broad frame but there was no one behind him in the hall.

"His footman came to the door."

"You may tell him I will be down momentarily," Adelia said. Richard nodded and the door had barely closed behind him when Lilah started to speak.

"Sending a footman up? What is he thinking?"

"Likely that it's a foggy night and he didn't want to bother with a mask."

"It's a slight," Lilah said. "Captain Lancaster always came up himself."

"Yes, well Captain Lancaster isn't a lord."

"And I like him all the better for it," Lilah said, handing Adelia her reticule and face mask.

Not wanting to keep the footman waiting, Adelia descended the stairs from her top floor apartment to the side entrance that was exclusively hers. She adjusted her red leather mask around her nose and mouth, gave Richard a nod, and stepped out to meet the waiting footman. It was too dark to get a good view of the steam carriage, but she could make out a gold monogram on the door, indicating it wasn't rented. The door opened and the footman handed her into the velvet lined interior and Adelia noted that Fletcher had left her the forward facing seat.

Apparently he could be a gentleman when he wished.

He was dressed in black, though he was wearing a striped cravat in shades of blue. His brown hair properly parted to one side, though it was perhaps a little long on top. Still, he was perfectly put together. As usual.

As the carriage moved, Adelia pulled off her mask, careful not to mess her hair.

"Thank you for picking me up in your carriage," she said, putting her mask into a bag embroidered in shades of red.

"I could hardly let you show up on your own. Not when we've so little time in which to establish our relationship."

"May I ask where we are going?"

"The Bombay Spectacle."

Adelia looked up from tying the drawstring on her bag. "Seriously?" Despite herself, her lips quirked in the faintest hint of a smile.

Fletcher straightened in his seat. "Why would I bother joking?"

"I meant no offense." Adelia finished tying the string and set her bag on the seat next to her. "I had assumed you'd choose something a little more … conventional. Perhaps a musical revue."

"Would you rather attend a revue?"

"Not at all," Adelia said in a quiet voice. She turned her attention to the small window, watching the glow from the gas lamp light up rusty clouds of fog.

The spectacle was the last place she'd expected Fletcher to take her, it was far too informal. He wouldn't be able to sit back and enjoy his brandy while the sycophants who crowded around waited for the great Lord's approval.

Though Adelia kept her eyes on the small window, as the carriage came to a stop she couldn't see much. It wasn't until the door opened and the footman helped her out that she got her first glimpse of the Bombay Spectacle.

In the past, circus acts had set up tents in empty fields around London, but that had come to an end after the factories had started running on aether energy. A tent was useless against the toxic London fog. However, the owners of one particular company had taken their inspiration from the circus of old and had built a permanent wooden structure that had the same dimensions as a tent.

The gravel pathway to the main entrance was lit by gas torches, illuminating the massive white structure towering over them. Adelia held her breath as she walked. It wasn't far enough that she wanted to bother with her mask, particularly when she'd noted Fletcher wasn't wearing his.

As they entered the great foyer, she let out the breath she'd been holding and was hit by the smell of earth. Beneath her feet was a packed dirt floor and to her right a line of men, women and children headed toward a ticket window.

"This way." Fletcher held out his arm and led her away from the line-up. They entered a hallway with a gold gate guarded by a stout automaton. Its squat body was painted in red and white stripes and black bowler hat topped off its round head. As they approached, Fletcher reached into a pocket in his jacket and withdrew a ticket. He tapped the automaton on the nose and its hinged mouth gaped open. It chomped down on the paper, it's bulbous eyes flicking from side to side before spitting the paper back out and opening the gate with a click.

"Where are we going?" Adelia asked as Fletcher led her down the hallway to a wooden staircase. It creaked slightly as they climbed.

"Have you never been here?"

"No, never."

"I can't believe Meri never took you."

Adelia felt the skin on the back of her neck heat. She wanted to point out that with Meri she'd never needed to parade around town like the day's latest catch.

"Captain Lancaster and I only went out occasionally and that was usually to dine."

"Well, you're in for a treat. There's nothing like the circus."

As they reached the top of the staircase, they came to a hallway lined with doors on the right hand side, each with a number painted in gold. Fletcher stopped in front of a door with the number five on it. Adelia could hear voices on the other side, laughing.

They were to be part of a group.

"Everything all right?" Fletcher asked, as though he'd sensed her hesitation.

Time to greet my audience, Adelia thought to herself as she pasted on a pleasant smile. "Of course, I'm very much looking forward to the show."

Fletcher looked as though he wanted to question her further, but instead knocked on the door. They were greeted by a footman who led them into an opulent boxed seating area with benches covered in red velvet. Two men and a woman were already lounging, drinks in hand.

The footman offered to take her cloak and Fletcher's hat. As she opened the clasp, revealing her ruby red gown, Adelia realized she perfectly matched her surroundings.

She handed over her cloak, noting Fletcher's eyes on her and she did a quick glance down at her dress to ensure everything was as it should be. Though the color was shocking, the cut itself was quite modest.

"What would you like to drink?" Fletcher leaned in so that his breath whispered over her skin. She fought the urge to tell him he was much too close. He'd obviously chosen the present company for a reason and she had to assume it had something to do with their ability to spread gossip.

"Champagne," Adelia said, her voice coming out in a whisper. "If you please."

Fletcher said something to the footman before offering his arm and leading her over to the guests. At their appearance, both men got to their feet.

"Fletch!" one of the men, a short man with a bullish build, called out. His pale blue eyes lit up when they landed on Adelia. "My my, who have we here?"

"Miss Adelia Dumont, may I introduce you to Mr. Clifford Townsend?" Fletcher said as Adelia held out her hand, forcing her smile to remain in place. Mr. Townsend brought her gloved fingers to his lips and lingered there.

"Aren't you just the jammiest bit of jam?"

Fletcher turned her toward the other gentleman, forcing Townsend to drop her hand. This man was thinner and taller and while Adelia thought he might be viewed as plain, there was a kindness in his eyes. "And this is Mr. Reginald Ives."

"Reggie, please." He took her hand briefly before focusing on her face. "I saw you in *Much Ado About Nothing* last year. Your performance was quite lovely."

"Come Reggie," the woman called from the bench. She was half reclined, making it difficult to tell just how tall she was. She wore a dress of jade silk that set off her black hair, though, the cut was much more daring than Adelia's. "I had no idea you were such a patron of the arts."

"And this is Miss Sophronia Lovejoy."

Obviously not a real name, Adelia thought to herself. *But who am I to judge?*

"Call me Ronnie," she said. "Everyone does."

"Lovely to meet you."

Ronnie straightened up and patted the seat next to her. "Sit with me while the gents catch up."

Adelia glanced in Fletcher's direction and noted that

he was already in conversation with Reggie. She extracted her arm from his hold and took a seat next to Ronnie. The benches were placed in such a way as to give an excellent view of the circus below. At the moment there was a pair of men juggling knives in the middle of a large ring. Across from the viewing boxes where her party was seated were stands filled with spectators, cheering them on as the knives soared through the air.

She noted that some of the crowd were just as focused on the well-dressed ladies and gentlemen in the boxes as they were on the act in the ring.

"Your champagne, Ma'am."

Adelia gave the footman a smile as she took her drink.

"So," Ronnie said, nodding at Fletcher, "how long have you two been … involved?"

Adelia brought her glass to her lips, barely sipping. "Not long, but it feels as though we've known each other for ages."

Ronnie let out a full-throated laugh. Though her accent was passable, Ronnie's manners would still mark her low birth. Not that such things mattered to Adelia.

"Can I ask how you and Lord Fletcher met?"

Ronnie shrugged an elegant shoulder, raising her empty glass to get the footman's attention. He immediately came over to take it, promising to return with a refill.

"Fletch and I met in the usual way, through common friends. I assume he snapped you up straight from the theater?"

Adelia forced a smile. "You could say that."

A creaking sound filled the arena and Ronnie leaned

over the edge of the box. "That's the clockwork animals coming."

The boards beneath their feet shook as a massive elephant entered the ring. It was at least as tall as two steam carriages stacked on top of each other. The creature jerked it's head from side to side, almost as though it could actually see the crowd. Following close behind, two clockwork tigers stalked into the arena.

"The first time Fletch brought me here, he took me down to see the clockworks up close after the show," Ronnie said. The footman had refreshed her drink and she was sipping a glass of deep red wine. "I'm sure he'll do the same for you if you ask."

Adelia felt a flash of annoyance and pretended to drink from her champagne glass. She knew what Ronnie was doing—Adelia had been around women like her frequently—and could tell when a woman was staking a prior claim. What she didn't understand was why Ronnie's actions bothered her. It wasn't like she and Fletcher were actually attached to each other. In fact, it was the very opposite.

It was probably a lingering side effect of the headache.

"Are you quite all right?" Ronnie asked. "You're rubbing your forehead."

It was then Adelia realized her temple was tingling. She was about to answer when her vision blurred. Gone were the brightly colored elephants and tigers. Gone was the chatter. Instead, she was in a room, a bedroom, with a silver handled brush in her hand.

"When will you accept this is over?"

She looked up to find Fletcher standing in front of her. But his clothes were different — he was in a brown coat.

"Surely you still care for me?" The words felt like they came from Adelia's lips, though they weren't words she'd ever say. She caught sight of a lock of black hair resting on her shoulder.

Fletcher frowned, a combination of distaste and confusion. "I could never care for someone like you."

The rush of the crowd came back and Adelia looked down at her hand but she was once again holding the champagne flute. Ronnie was clapping in delight, completely engrossed in the tigers below. Adelia noticed the woman's black hair, the way it curled over one shoulder. She brought her glass to her lips, draining it.

Fletcher watched Adelia as she leaned forward, her eyes fixed on the exotic mechanical elephants and tigers entering the ring. This more than anything else was what the Bombay Spectacle was known for.

Having seen the show before, Fletcher found he was much more interested in Adelia's reaction. In fact, he'd been most interested in her reactions all evening.

She was something of an enigma, but then, perhaps that was to be expected from an actress.

As he watched her he couldn't help but notice the contrast between her and Ronnie, not only in their manners, but also their bearing. Fletcher noted that while Adelia's red dress drew the eye, the cut was on the modest side. In fact, he'd seen debutantes with lower necklines.

"She's quite a treat, isn't she?" Clifford was practically licking his lips as he watched Adelia's delighted smile when the mechanic got the elephant up on it's back legs. "You're a lucky dog. How'd you snag her?"

"We met backstage." That was the truth at least. "She couldn't resist my charms."

"More like your coin," Clifford snorted. "I've got a fair amount myself now that my uncle has passed on. Perhaps when you're done with her, you could put in a word for me?"

Fletcher's stomach twisted and he had a pressing urge to force his friend to shut his face.

"Are you all right?" Reggie asked, seeing something in Fletcher's demeanor that Clifford hadn't.

"Yes, of course." Fletcher finished his brandy. He was behaving rather stupidly. After all, these were the sorts of statements Clifford often made.

"How's your mother?" Reggie asked.

Fletcher knew his friend was trying to change the subject, but bringing his mother up wasn't likely to relax him.

"She's her usual charming self."

"Still pushing you to marry?"

Fletcher laughed. "She's got a lady in mind but I'm hoping for a reprieve."

"Ah, in what guise?"

"The fair Adelia is bound for Ireland on tour with her company. I'm hoping to convince her to take pity on me and bring me along."

"I had wondered at your haste in taking a mistress," Reggie said. "Considering you haven't settled on one la-dybird in years."

"But now it makes sense?"

Reggie looked from Fletcher to Adelia. "Yes, I rather think it does."

The screeching roar of the tiger drew Fletcher's attention back to the ring and he watched as the clockwork beast hopped through a ring of fire, it's metal legs creaking from the exertion. No one would ever mistake the stilted movements for a real animal, but if the tremendous applause were anything to go by, the audience didn't care.

"Is Miss Dumont quite all right?"

At Reggie's question, Fletcher glanced over to see Adelia rubbing her temple with her gloved fingers. Did she look a bit pale?

"I imagine she's tired. She finished a run last evening."

The main act was finishing up and they'd done what they needed to do. Fletcher asked the footman to fetch Adelia's cloak. Time to go home and let the gossip mill do its work.

CHAPTER FIVE

Adelia paced back and forth in her small sitting room, waiting for the doctor's arrival. Lilah had sent a message when Adelia had admitted that her symptoms had gotten worse. Unfortunately, Dr. Sahni had been out of town for a few days but she'd made arrangements to see Adelia as soon as she'd returned—much to Adelia's tremendous relief. She'd begun to fear she wouldn't get to see the doctor before her trip to Ireland.

Adelia knew Fletcher had been watching her after the brief episode she'd had the night of the spectacle, but luckily he hadn't pushed her when she'd explained she was feeling tired. Instead he'd told her that they'd accomplished what they needed to and had brought her back home.

Which, Adelia had to admit, had been rather chivalrous of him.

In fact, he'd been nothing but polite each time he'd taken her out since. Luckily she hadn't had another vision, but the tingling in her head had become more and more frequent. Fortunately Mr. Davis had agreed to let Fletcher travel with the company to Ireland, and Adelia had convinced Fletcher that she needed a few days to herself to prepare for the trip.

"Miss?" Lilah broke through her thoughts. "Dr. Sahni is here."

"Show her right in."

Calling on her training in the theater, Adelia came to stand beside a wingback chair, taking deep breaths so she'd appear calm once the doctor made it up to her third floor apartment.

Lilah opened the door, announcing the guest's arrival.

In her mid to late twenties and wearing a peacock blue day dress and jacket, Dr. Sahni didn't look like any other physician Adelia had ever seen. It was probably for the best considering no other medical professional had ever given her proper treatment.

As she stepped into Adelia's rose and gold sitting room, the doctor handed her bonnet to Lilah, her jet black hair neatly pinned back. She opened her reticule, taking out a pair of spectacles and looked Adelia over from head to toe with warm brown eyes.

Definitely not like other doctors.

"If you could bring us a tray, Lilah?" Adelia asked.

Her maid dropped a quick curtsy before heading off to the kitchen and Adelia invited the doctor to sit.

"I was surprised by the urgency of your message," Dr. Sahni said, taking a seat on the settee closest to Adelia's chair. "Our recent visits seem to have been quite unremarkable."

"I appreciate your making time to see me." Adelia clutched her hands on her lap. "I had an episode. Or, at least, I think I did."

"You aren't certain?"

"It happened quickly. It couldn't have lasted even half a minute."

"You've been taking your blockers regularly?"

Adelia nodded. "I never miss one."

"And when did the symptoms first reappear?"

"It started as a headache. I thought I was tired—we just finished a run of *Macbeth*."

"I saw one of your performances. You were flawless, as always."

"Thank you." Adelia forced a tight smile. "The headache dissipated, but there was a tingling sensation left behind. Then, when I was out last week it was much worse."

"How so?"

Adelia thought back to the spectacle, to the elephant display and how her mind seemed to wander out of her body and into that of the woman seated next to her.

"You'll think I'm a lunatic," Adelia's voice grew quiet.

Dr. Sahni frowned. "You've been seeing me long enough to know that I never speak in those terms, not about girls like you."

Adelia let out a breath. "Of course, I meant no disrespect. I'm having a hard time processing the experience."

Lilah arrived with the tea tray and Adelia used the reprieve while the maid poured two cups of tea to get her thoughts in order.

"Drink something," the doctor pointed at Adelia's teacup and scooped in extra sugar as Lilah left, closing the drawing room door behind her. "You look far too pale."

Adelia sipped her tea, grateful for the added sweetness, and began to recount the episode. Dr. Sahni didn't interrupt her once, allowing her to finish her story and even taking a moment to reflect before speaking.

"Would you say that this vision you had felt real?"

Adelia nodded. "I could feel the brush in my hand. It's the aether fever, isn't it? I've not had an episode in years, not since I found you, but that's what it feels like."

The doctor set down her teacup and leaned forward, assessing Adelia's face. "When do you turn twenty-one?"

"In the spring," Adelia answered. "Is that relevant?"

"I have noticed that some of my patients have experienced an increase in symptoms this year, in the lead up to their twenty-first birthday. I don't have a large enough sample to draw definitive conclusions, but I believe that's what you are experiencing."

"So the fever is back?" Adelia's hands trembled and tea splashed over her dress before she could set her cup down.

"There's no reason to worry. I've never been given any reason to suspect that the visions associated with the fever are in any way harmful."

"Perhaps not physically, but if I were to draw attention to myself I'm certain my career would be over."

"Indeed. I will adjust your dosage, but I want to check in with you in a week to see how it's working."

"I'm to leave for Ireland in two days," Adelia said. "This couldn't have happened at a worse time."

"There's no way to postpone the tour?"

If she were going for herself, Adelia might have considered sending an understudy, but under the circumstances, there was no way to find another agent to take her place.

"I'm afraid I cannot."

"Then I recommend you find a companion, one you can trust to help you if a vision catches you unaware."

She would have to confide in Lilah. Fletcher could not, under any circumstances, find out about the fever.

"There is no way to stop the visions?"

"Not without prescribing *persephamine*," Dr. Sahni wrinkled her nose as she said the word. "And the side effects are worse than the cure."

Adelia had known several girls to take the drug in the past. While it prevented visions, it had left the girls listless and some cases nearly catatonic. Definitely not something Adelia would ever consider.

"There is one further development I need to discuss with you," Dr. Sahni hesitated, placing her cup down on the table in front of her. "Some women have reported strange correlations around their visions. Coincidences if you will."

Adelia was glad she wasn't holding her tea any longer as her dress would surely be ruined.

"What sort of correlations?"

"The kind that gives these women reason to believe their visions might be real—that what they experience is in fact something that has actually happened and they are seeing it through someone else's eyes."

"You're serious?"

Dr. Sahni straightened in her chair, a wariness in her eyes. "I am telling you this because it is my policy to give my patients all the facts as I know them. In this case, while it might sound inconceivable, I have had reports of women having visions that have come to pass. Or in some cases, visions about things that have already happened."

"But, surely that's not possible?"

Dr. Sahni gave her a weak smile that didn't reach her eyes. "I cannot be certain, but my advice to you is to take care and protect yourself."

Fletcher had left his packing to Myles, an action he was starting to regret as he looked through the items his valet had strewn across his dressing room.

"Your trunk is ready to go," Myles said, entering the room with a black evening jacket over his arm.

"Do you think so?" Fletcher asked, waving a hand at the disarray surrounding them. "If that's the case then surely it's the only thing ready."

"This won't take even an hour to reorganize." Myles held the jacket out. "All will be in order by the time you return from dinner."

Fletcher put on the jacket and waited while Myles adjusted his cravat. What his valet lacked in organizing ability, he more than made up for in his enthusiasm around tying knots.

"I don't like the white," Myles said, taking a step back to look at his handiwork. "It's so old fashioned."

"So is my mother," Fletcher said. "And she insists on a white cravat for formal dinners."

"Speaking of Lady Fletchingham, a maid came by with the message that your mother wanted a word with you before dinner this evening."

Fletcher imagined she wanted several.

"She said you should meet her in the drawing room before your guests arrive."

"Very well." He gave himself a once over in the mirror and decided he looked good enough. It wasn't like his mother wouldn't find something to criticize if she'd already made up her mind to do it.

"I'll just get on this dressing room after I have my supper then, will I?" Myles called after Fletcher.

"Did you arrange to dine with the maids again?"

Myles grinned. "They love my company, what can I say?"

Fletcher waved him off, leaving his suite of rooms, and heading down the hall to the main staircase.

Wilson was stationed in the foyer, the shine of his shoes second only to the shine on the marble floor. It was apparent his mother was set on impressing. Dozens of candles burned in brass holders. Lady Fletchingham refused to allow gas lamps saying they could well afford to replace the wax each day. Fletcher disagreed, saying it was a waste of the servants' time to constantly remove candles, but it was an argument that held little weight with his mother.

He slowed his pace as he approached the open drawing room doors where the soapy scent of hot house lilies clung to the air. His mother stood at a side table near the fireplace, fixing an arrangement in a massive crystal vase. She wore a deep green evening gown, again accompanied by diamonds.

As Fletcher entered the room she looked him over from head to toe.

"Your hair needs a trim."

"Is that why you wished to speak with me?" He moved toward her, stopping next to the fireplace and resting an elbow on the mantle. There was fire going but it did little to add warmth to the room.

Lady Fletchingham turned her attention back to the flowers, picking out a calla lily and moving it to the front.

"I heard a rumor that you were considering leaving town."

"It's hardly a rumor," Fletcher said. "I'm booked on an airship in two days' time."

In reality it had been easy to convince Mr. Davis to extend him an invitation. He'd barely even hinted at wanting to accompany Adelia when the arrangements were made for him to replace Meri.

"You gave me your word that you would consider marriage this season."

"And I plan to," Fletcher said. "As soon as I get all my affairs in order."

"Affairs indeed. Do you think I don't hear the rumors? I know about you and the actress."

Of course she did, Fletcher thought to himself. He'd been out with Adelia three times in the past week, always in very public places. It was too much to hope the gossip which he'd needed to reach the ears of Mr. Davis wouldn't also worm its way to his mother.

Lady Fletchingham took a step back, eyeing the arrangement, then she picked out the calla lily again. "You can hardly court a proper lady—a debutante no less—while you are running about with an actress."

"An announcement is hardly forthcoming. I told you I would give Lady Fianna proper consideration."

"Excellent. Then you will be staying in town."

"No, I told you, I have some affairs to attend to. I'll be back in a fortnight."

Lady Fletchingham snapped the stalk of the lily and threw it into the grate. Fletcher watched as the flower dissolved into flames. "Your father and I expected better of you."

Fletcher felt his face heat as anger threatened to overtake him and it took all his energy to force it down. His mother would see any show of emotion as a sign of weakness and it wasn't as though they would never agree on what it meant to honor his father's memory anyway.

The sound of a carriage hissing to a stop cut off all further discussion. Fletcher had rarely been so eager to play the host. "I believe I hear our guests arriving. We can continue this conversation when I return from Ireland."

Lady Fletchingham raised her eyebrow, a determined gleam in her eye. "One can hope you'll be of a more dutiful disposition at that time."

CHAPTER SIX

"I can't believe we have to dine in," Captain Merritt "Meri" Lancaster said, picking up his wine glass. The candlelight caught his gold-blond hair, giving him an almost ethereal look, though his features were far from cherubic. With his strong jaw and warm chestnut brown eyes, Meri would make an excellent avenging angel. Though, at this moment he looked more than a little petulant.

"Is my cook really so bad?" Adelia asked, eyeing his empty plate. They were seated in the small dining area, just off her drawing room. "I know she's not as fancy as you are used to, but I'm quite attached to her."

"Of course not, but it does feel as though we're in hiding."

Adelia watched the light reflect off the red wine in her glass. After her encounter with Dr. Sahni, Meri's arrival was a welcome reprieve from all thoughts of the fever. "In a way we are. It hardly helps our case, now that we've got the gossips convinced that I'm seeing Lord Fletcher, for me to appear on your arm."

"I understand the logic," Meri said, the corners of his mouth pulling up into a wistful smile, "but I'm still sore about not getting to take my leave in Ireland."

"Are you permitted to tell me why your leave was cancelled?" Adelia rarely asked Meri for specific details about his work as a naval officer, but his leave had been terminated so suddenly, she couldn't help but be curious.

His lips formed a grim line. "Unfortunately the reason is classified."

"That sounds interesting."

"I assure you it is not."

"At least you're stationed in London again. That must make your mother happy."

"Indeed. She had me accompany my sisters to a soiree hosted by Lady Germaine."

"Sounds fancy."

"It was exceedingly dull."

Adelia laughed. "Did you have to fend off any suitors?"

"With their poor dowries? Hardly." Meri's lips pulled into a frown. "Let's talk about something else. How about your mission?"

"You already know all about it," Adelia said. "You were supposed to come with me."

"Why am I getting the distinct impression that you are displeased with the switch?"

The door to the salon opened and Cassie, the part-time maid who helped Lilah, poked her head in. "Shall I clear the table?"

"Yes, please," Adelia said, knowing the sooner the dishes were done, the sooner Cassie could retire for the evening.

Once the table was cleared and they were left with just

their wine glasses, Meri tapped his finger on the surface of the table.

"You didn't answer my question."

"What question was that?"

"You don't like Fletcher."

"That's not a question."

Meri smirked. "Fine. Why don't you like Fletcher?"

"I don't know Lord Fletcher well enough to either like or dislike him."

"Delia darling," Meri said, drawing out her nickname. "You are an excellent actress."

"Thank you."

"But you cannot fool me. What is it about Fletcher? Is it because he tried to proposition you when you first met?"

Adelia scowled. "I only told you that story because you promised we'd never have to discuss it again."

"Surely he wasn't the first man to make you a distasteful offer?"

"Of course not."

"And you told me he didn't press when you made your feelings clear?"

"No, he did not."

"Then why continue to hold it against him?"

Adelia opened her mouth to answer, but shut it again. Meri always did know how to stump her. But he raised an interesting question. Why did she hold Fletcher's past actions against him?

He'd been nothing but a gentleman since then, despite the fact they'd been actively trying to convince everyone she was his mistress. After their evening at the circus she'd even started to think he wasn't all bad.

But then there'd been her appointment with Dr. Sahni. If the doctor was indeed correct and her visions were true, then that meant she had seen something that had really happened between Fletcher and Miss Lovejoy.

I could never care for someone like you.

Such cold words for someone he'd obviously been in a relationship with. Given Ronnie's low birth though, was it really surprising? He was an aristocrat after all.

Adelia didn't need Fletcher's admiration, but she did need his respect.

"Perhaps it's because I have to work with him," she said, choosing her words with care. "You don't know what it's like to have a professional relationship with a man who sees you as a bunter."

Meri frowned and shook his head. "Fletcher isn't like that. His friends come from all circles."

"His male friends perhaps."

"None of us have many female friends, but it might help you to know that Fletcher's the one who recommended you for the agency."

Adelia nearly knocked over her wine glass, but she caught it just in time. "Don't be ridiculous. You're the one who recruited me."

She remembered it clearly. Meri had come right up to her after a performance of *The Taming of the Shrew* and told her he had a perfect part for her.

Which was when he'd told her about Her Majesty's Secret Agency.

"I did that under Fletcher's direction."

"Pardon?" There was no way she'd heard him properly.

"Fletcher was the one who had the idea to recruit you."

The headache she'd finally gotten under control a few days ago was threatening to come back.

"Why didn't you tell me this before now?"

Meri's lips quirked but he knew better than to smile. "You have never been particularly accommodating to conversations regarding Lord Fletcher."

Adelia sipped her wine. Then she sipped it again. "Is this why you insisted on having dinner before I left town? To convince me of Lord Fletcher's virtues and save him from my sour moods?"

"You never have sour moods," Meri said, though his expression turned serious. "Actually, there was something else I wanted to talk to you about."

He reached into his inside jacket pocket and took out a small framed miniature, resting it on the table between them. Adelia picked it up for a closer look. A pretty young woman with dark hair and eyes looked out of the delicate frame.

"Is this your sweetheart?"

"Hardly. That's the sister of a fellow officer. Her name is Mariah Cohen and she went missing about six months ago."

"She was at Cravenwood?"

"She was but she went missing a month before Hazel's rescue efforts. Would you keep an eye out for her?"

"I will. Can I keep this?" She held up the miniature.

Meri nodded. "You will be careful? I know Fletcher will keep an eye on you, but this mission could get tangly if you discover where the girls are being kept."

"Do you think we can actually find them?"

"The source of our information is unconventional, but I trust it. You'll need to keep an eye out for resort towns, especially ones near a harbor. Or at least Fletcher will. Your main job is to distract everyone on stage so no one notices what he's about."

Adelia nodded. "I'll keep it in mind."

"You didn't answer me about being careful."

"I can look out for myself, but if it makes you feel better, I'll keep an eye out for Lord Fletcher as well."

Meri raised his glass. "I expect nothing less."

Of course his mother had him seated next to Lady Fianna through a six-course dinner. He wasn't sure if he'd ever spent so much time in conversation with a debutant and he hoped never to be in such a position again.

She was a pretty girl with blond curls and blue eyes. The pale pink dress she wore set off her complexion nicely and she held herself with poise and grace. She had obviously been well prepared for her come-out.

"Have you been enjoying your first season?" Fletcher asked.

Lady Fianna didn't immediately answer. She cast her eyes down, her long lashes fanning over her cheeks. She was a beautiful young woman, he couldn't fault his mother there. He just wished they had something to talk about.

"Everyone has been most kind," Fianna answered, finally looking up at him with her clear blue eyes. "I've been invited to so many engagements, Mama said we couldn't possibly attend everything even in two seasons."

Fletcher reached for his wine glass, glancing in the direction of the waiters who were arriving with the next course.

"Did you enjoy Lady Germaine's ball?" Fianna asked. "It was my very first event of the season."

"I cannot recall much about it."

"You were kind enough to dance with me."

Fletcher drained his wine glass, wishing for something stronger.

"Of course I remember our dance," Fletcher said, wracking his brain for any recollection of that night. He remembered dancing with Lady Hazel because she made him laugh but the rest of the evening was a blur.

While Fianna cut her fish into small pieces Fletcher was once again grasping for some topic of discussion. "Do you have any hobbies?"

Fianna put her fork down, thinking over the question. "I enjoy playing the pianoforte. I've also been learning the art of flower arranging."

Fletcher caught the footman's attention and his wine was refilled. He could feel his mother's eyes on him but he picked up his glass anyway.

"Of course, now that I've come out into society I don't have as much time for practice. I've been fortunate in making a number of friendships with superior young ladies."

"She certainly has," her mother, Countess Sinclair spoke up. "Lady Carmella Barton has taken a particular interest in Fianna and has introduced her to a number of the members of the League of Ladies."

Despite their former leader—Lady Ashburn's—fall from grace as an alleged kidnapper, the League of Ladies had quickly recovered, putting the young Lady Carmella in place as their leader and surrounding her with ladies from all the best families.

Fletcher's head filled with images of coming home from his club and finding his drawing room overflowing with the sort of ladies he'd spent the last eight years avoiding.

He gave himself a mental shake. Husbands and wives usually kept separate lives. If he and Lady Fianna married he need not have anything to do with her friends or her hobbies.

The thought should have made him happy, or at the very least relieved, but instead he was filled with a heaviness. He reached for his wine glass and drained it again.

CHAPTER SEVEN

Adelia stood at the port barely an hour after sunrise with Lilah and two trunks. It was still early and so far the sun rays held off the fog, though she could see it starting to creep up, around her feet. They'd need to either board soon, or put on their masks.

A black and gold airship sat in the water in front of them with a crew of men working to set up the gangplank.

"Are you sure it's safe?" Lilah asked, eyeing the balloon that loomed above them, easily twice the size of the schooner.

"It's as safe as any form of transport over water can be."

"That isn't reassuring," Lilah said.

The other members of the theater troupe trickled toward the dock and chatted in excited groups around her, waiting for boarding. Adelia considered approaching some of her friends when a navy blue steam carriage pulled up.

"Lilah, would you find someone to take care of loading our trunks?" Adelia asked as she watched Fletcher alight from the carriage with an attractive young man with dark curly hair trailing him as he headed her way.

"Good morning, Miss Dumont," Fletcher said, sweeping into a bow as he stopped in front of her. He wore shades of brown this morning which, on anyone else should have looked dull but instead brought out the bronze tone to his brown hair and eyes. "I trust you are well rested despite the hour?"

"I am, thank you."

It was true. It had only been a few days, but the extra blockers Dr. Sahni had prescribed seemed to be working. Though, Adelia had been warned it would be several days before she would know if the dosage needed an adjustment.

At that moment Lilah returned alone with a frown on her face. Adelia noted that the young man at Fletcher's side perked up at the appearance of the maid, pushing his curly dark hair out of his eyes so he could get a better look. For her part, Lilah was entirely focused on the trunks.

"I was unable to find any spare crewman," Lilah said, her eyes still wandering the docks. "You should board and I'll wait here to see that the trunks are properly loaded."

"I can stay with you," Fletcher's manservant stepped forward, then appeared to remember his place, glancing at his employer. "Assuming that's all right with you, my lord."

"Yes Myles, and perhaps you can see to it that my trunk also arrives on board?"

The man grinned at Fletcher's dry tone and Adelia made up her mind that she quite liked Myles.

"Shall we?" Fletcher held out his left arm to Adelia

and she placed her hand on his elbow, allowing him to lead her up the gangway.

"Have you been aboard an airship before?" Adelia asked as she tried not to focus on the fact that the boards beneath her feet did not feel all that solid. One of the differences between an airship and a seabound vessel was the need for more levels below deck, since passengers rarely spent much time above. This meant the trek up the gangway was a little longer, since the deck was higher.

"As a matter of fact I have, and quite recently too."

Adelia was about to ask him for more details when she realized they'd reached the main deck. A man in a black and gold uniform helped her aboard and then led them to a narrow staircase to the main seating area. The gold theme continued here, accenting the black leather seats arranged in two rows with a red carpeted aisle down the middle. Gold and crystal chandeliers hung from the ceiling but the main source of light came from the windows lining both sides.

Within the rows, the seats were arranged in facing pairs and several groups had already claimed places on both sides of the aisle.

"Adelia!" Albert Knowles, Adelia's favorite leading man, called for her attention. "Who's your friend?"

The very last thing Adelia wanted to do was to talk to Bertie about Fletcher. As one of her oldest friends, he'd have no trouble seeing through her false relationship.

"Bertie, this is Lord Fletcher. My lord, this is Albert Knowles, a fellow actor."

"I saw you in *Julius Caesar*," Fletcher said. "Your Marc Antony is without comparison."

Bertie lit up. "Thank you, my lord. It's one of my favorite parts."

"We should find seats," Adelia said. "I think we're taking off soon."

"Yes, of course," Bertie said, turning his attention to Adelia. "We'll talk later, yeah?"

She knew it wasn't really a question, but at least she'd have some time to prepare for his actual questions.

Fletcher led the way to an empty seating area and Adelia settled next to a window.

"Have you ever been on an airship?" He asked, taking the seat across from her.

"No, I've done some short tours in Scotland and Northern England, but we always travelled by carriage."

Just as she finished speaking, the floor beneath their feet began to rumble.

"Preparing for take-off," Fletcher said. "It won't be long now."

"I hope Lilah made it aboard." Adelia looked out the window with a frown. Unfortunately she was seated on the harborside.

"If it will set your mind at ease, I'll go check."

"Thank you, I think it would."

After checking below deck and finding Lilah not only safely aboard, but also seeming to be happily on the receiving end of Myles' attentions, he went back up to the first class passenger area, when he noted that Adelia had been joined by Mr. Davis. The man had even taken Fletcher's seat, leaving him to sit in the chair next to Adelia.

He noted that Adelia had a bland, though pleasant expression while Davis spoke about the theater they were set to perform in during their time in Belfast.

"It's the first time a company has been granted a visa to go farther than Dublin," Davis said, his voice full of enthusiasm. "I think it shows how much faith the government has in our company, letting us travel so close to the West-Irish border. And did I tell you that the British ambassador to Ireland may come see us?"

"It would be quite an honor," Adelia said, tapping her gloved fingers against the book in her lap. Fletcher caught just the faintest hint of derision in her tone. She was mocking Davis but he was so entranced by her easy smile that the man had no idea.

A jerking motion had Adelia clutching the armrest between them, her fingers just barely brushing Fletcher's arm. She turned her attention to the window.

"We're rising," she said, her voice pitching higher as she rested her forehead against the glass. Sitting next to her, Fletcher was certain her excitement was genuine. "It's so loud."

As the ship drew out of the water, the sound of the engines was no longer muffled.

"It'll settle soon," Fletcher said, raising his voice over the noise. "Once we're at peak altitude."

Adelia nodded at him, turning her attention back to the window.

Seeing that his star's attention was otherwise engaged, and perhaps knowing no one could hear him anyway, Davis excused himself.

With the seats in front of them empty, Fletcher

stretched his legs out. It was poor manners, but his mother wasn't here to correct him and it made for a slightly
more comfortable journey.

It was odd, but this airship trip would be the most
time he and Adelia had yet to spend alone in only each
other's company. Their outings around London had been
very public, with the only time they'd been alone being
while in his carriage, en route to some event.

After several more minutes watching out the window,
Adelia settled back against her seat. A young woman in a
black skirt and white blouse with a black and gold beret
came by to take their orders.

"Can I get you anything?"

Adelia requested coffee and Fletcher ordered a brandy. As the server went to get his drink, he could feel Adelia's eyes on him.

"Is everything all right?" Fletcher asked.

"I'm not sure." Adelia furrowed her brow. "It's barely
full morning."

"I had noticed."

"And you ordered a brandy."

"Your powers of observation are astute."

The line between her brows deepened, but she didn't
say anything, instead opening the book in her lap as the
server returned. Fletcher perked up when he caught the
title: *The Long Walk to Midnight*. It was a mystery novel
he'd read a month ago.

"Have you read *The Stalking Hour*?" Fletcher asked. "It
came out last year."

Adelia looked up from the page she was reading. "I've
read all of D.A. Fitzgerald's books. Or at least all the ones

I can find. Are you an admirer of theirs?"

"I enjoy a good mystery story."

"Then you must have read the novels of Sir Garett Jones."

Fletcher grinned. "I not only read them, I've met him. He's a member of my club."

Adelia dropped the book into her lap. "Did you ask him about the ending to *Stranger from the North*?"

They spent the next hour talking about books they'd read and it wasn't until the server came by again that Fletcher realized he hadn't touched his brandy.

CHAPTER EIGHT

As the airship descended Adelia was still coming to terms with the fact that a journey that would have taken hours by sea, was being completed in the matter of a morning. It also helped that she and Fletcher had passed much of the time discussing books.

Fletcher was courteous as they disembarked, tracking down Lilah and Myles and their trunks.

Adelia had learned that their first day in Belfast was to be spent acclimatising to the city. Ireland as a whole might be divided politically—with the east professing loyalty to the Crown and the west being neutral—but one thing the country did agree on was limited use of aether. There were no steam carriages, no factories piping smoke into the atmosphere, and airships were such a rarity that the docks were crowded with onlookers as they disembarked from the ship.

Which meant that even when it was an overcast day, the air was still clean and clear.

After settling Adelia and Lilah into a horse-drawn carriage, Fletcher and Myles had gone to secure their trunks.

"I can't believe we don't need to wear masks here," Lilah said, twisting her head out the open carriage window in an attempt to see the horses again. "Do you think we're safe with those animals?"

In all honesty, Adelia had no idea. Having grown up in and around London, her exposure to horses had been quite limited to the few interactions she'd had while on country tours. But at least she'd been in a horse-drawn carriage before, unlike her maid.

"I'm certain it's fine," Adelia said. "They must be quite well-trained—look at how nicely they are waiting for the driver's instructions."

Lilah wrinkled her nose. "I'm not sure that they smell better than the steam carriages, but still, the airship ride alone was more than enough for me. I'm so glad I came to work for you instead of a lady."

As soon as the words were out, Lilah clapped a hand over her mouth. "I meant no disrespect—"

"I'm not offended." Adelia cut her off with a wave. She'd long ago come to terms with her place in society. There were very few things that could cause her offense anymore.

Fletcher chose that moment to join them in the carriage with Myles jumping into the empty seat next to him. If the young man's wide-eyed wonder were anything to go by, he was equally impressed by the horses.

"They're magnificent," Myles said as the carriage jolted forward. "Absolute beasts."

"To think men ride them," Lilah said, leaning forward.

"And some women," Fletcher added.

They closed the carriage windows as they began the short journey to their accommodations. While there was no aether in the air, Belfast was still a city filled with horse-drawn carriages.

Myles and Lilah continued their banter back and forth and Adelia was relieved that Fletcher didn't seem overly stuffy with his servants. Adelia had always been friend-ly with her assistants and maids. Considering her back-ground, there'd never been any point in putting on airs and she found people were generally pleased to help her when she showed them kindness in return.

At least, that was her experience with women. With men she'd learned to keep her guard up.

The carriage rolled to a stop in front of the Hotel Donegall, their home for the next two weeks. Fletcher dis-mounted first and held out a hand to help Adelia down. Lilah and Myles followed, heading off to find the trunks while Adelia and Fletcher were invited to afternoon tea in the hotel's grand drawing room.

All Adelia wanted was quiet. Spending her evenings surrounded by people at the theater, she preferred the peace of her apartment for a few hours during the day. But there would be no such reprieve until their rooms were ready.

"We'll be sharing a suite on the top floor," Adelia said in a low voice as they followed a line of actors up the wide sandstone steps leading up to the grand entrance. "Mr. Davis upgraded me when he knew I'd be in such exalted company."

"How will you endure the attention?" Fletcher's lips quirked when he asked the question and Adelia found herself smiling back.

"With the good grace that has made me a household name throughout London, my lord."

Fletcher actually laughed as they entered the main main foyer.

The first thing that struck Adelia was the color, or lack thereof. Everything was white. An enormous crystal chandelier hung from the ceiling, draped in strands of pearls. The floor was white tile with a high polish. Even the wide staircase had a white carpet runner. Keeping the space clean must have required its own full time staff.

Adelia noted that her troupe mates were no less impressed than she was, their heads turning as they followed a footman into a main floor drawing room. Only Fletcher remained impassive, but then she assumed he was used to such grandeur.

While not completely white, the drawing room had the same polished floor and a similar style of chandelier, though on a smaller scale. The furnishings and curtains in this room were black velvet, providing a stark, but elegant contrast.

Fletcher led her to an empty settee. "I'll return with some refreshments. Is there anything in particular you'd like?"

"I'm not fond of custard, but anything else would be fine."

Fletcher stopped. "I'm sorry, did you say you aren't fond of custard?"

"Yes."

"What about tarts?"

"If they have custard tarts, then no."

"I think you've never had the right custard."

"I think such a thing doesn't exist."

Fletcher shook his head as he walked away and Adelia settled on the settee.

"Isn't this grand?"

Adelia looked up to see Renata Rose, a pretty young woman with large brown eyes and masses of chestnut hair come to stand next to the settee. "Do you mind if I join you?"

"Not at all," Adelia said. While she had been enjoying her solitude, there were much worse companions than Renata. Like Adelia she was an actress, though she was still working her way up to a starring role. She'd joined the tour as Adelia's understudy, which was a definite promotion, though she'd still likely spend her time in the background scenes and helping out backstage with props.

She was keen though. Always looking for acting advice or to help Adelia run lines.

"Did you enjoy the airship?" Adelia asked.

"Oh yes," Renanta's smile was genuine. Though she and Adelia were only a year or so apart in age, Renata had maintained a sense of youthful innocence that Adelia had lost long ago.

They chatted about the trip until Fletcher returned, at which time Renata excused herself, though not without giving the gentleman a once over behind his back. Based on the gleam in her eye Adelia could only assume that her friend liked what she saw.

After tea, Adelia went up to their suite of rooms while

Fletcher remained in the drawing room, allowing her time to get settled. He took a cup of coffee to the window, looking out over the city. Like London, it was often overcast and foggy, but there was no tinge of red in the mist here.

Normally his afternoons were tied up with Agency work. More often than not he'd be at Burke's Club where he'd sip brandy, making the occasional bets, playing the role of a gentleman of extreme idleness, all the while discussing matters of national security in back rooms with the other agents.

"My Lord."

Fletcher looked up to see Mr. Davis approaching him with a well dressed reddish haired man at his side.

"I wondered if I could introduce you to Mr. James Morrissey? His father owns the theater here and James was pivotal in setting up the tour on this end."

"Nice to meet you, Mr. Morrissey," Fletcher said with a nod.

"James, please," the young man flashed a smile. His Irish accent wasn't thick, but it was present enough to give a lilt to his words. "I hope your voyage was pleasant?"

"Air travel generally is," Fletcher agreed. "So civilized."

"We rarely have ships come to port," James continued. "Your arrival was quite an event."

Fletcher sipped his coffee, wishing for all the world it was a brandy. He hated inane socializing. At least, he hated it while completely sober. He set his cup down and went back to observing James. The young man was pleasant and unassuming, with easy manners. It made it difficult to get a read on him.

Davis and James soon moved on and Fletcher abandoned his coffee. He glanced at his pocket watch. He'd given Adelia three quarters of an hour to get settled. It was time for them to discuss strategy.

Their suite was located on the third floor and Fletcher noted there was only one other door on their floor. At least they'd have enough space to keep out of each other's way. He entered a spacious drawing room which, unlike the rest of the hotel he'd seen, had been infused with color. Or at least a color. The furnishings, curtains and carpeting were shades of soft, gray blue. Though white dominated the walls and the marble fireplace.

The room was large enough that it had a nook with a round table for dining in and a separate seating area near the fireplace for entertaining. There was a doorway on each side of the room which he assumed led to their separate chambers. Myles appeared from the door to Fletcher's left.

"My lord," Myles nodded. "Is there anything I can do for you?"

"Is Miss Dumont about?"

"Her maid said she needed a few hours to prepare for tomorrow, for rehearsals."

Fletcher glanced at his pocket watch. There was no point wasting the afternoon. "In that case, I'm going out."

CHAPTER NINE

Adelia slept poorly, likely due to the change in surroundings, but as was her habit, she was up early the next morning.

The show would be opening in two days and there was no time to lose if the cast wanted to get in a proper run-through in the Belfast theater.

"A simple day dress is fine," Adelia told Lilah. "It's barely two blocks from here to the theater."

After dressing, Adelia sat in the small sitting room outside her chamber. Though the rooms weren't as large as her apartment in London, Adelia had enough space on her side of the suite that she felt she could comfortably spend all her time there. It wasn't that she wanted to completely avoid Fletcher, but sharing an apartment with a man was awkward enough. It was best they keep to their own spaces.

Lilah had arranged for a breakfast tray to be brought up and Adelia had sat next to a window, sipping tea and reviewing her lines one last time.

"Should I accompany you?" Lilah asked as Adelia prepared to leave.

"I'll be fine on my own. There's no need to change our routine because we are in a new city."

"As you wish, Miss."

Though the sky was overcast, Adelia took a moment to pause on the street in front of the hotel. The air wasn't exactly fresh, though she assumed no city was, with so many people living so closely together, but the lack of aether in the air was a welcome sensation.

Heading toward the theater, Adelia wasn't surprised to run into Renata walking with Millie's first assistant, a round cheeked woman named Beulah. Adelia fell into step with the two women and they walked together.

"Are you enjoying the accommodations?" Renata asked.

"I am," Adelia said. "It's better than I could have hoped for."

"I suppose it pays to travel with a lord," Beulah said, and while Adelia knew she meant the comment in jest, her chest still tightened in dread. She hated being the source of company chatter and because of her supposed affair with Lord Fletcher, she was most assuredly the source of much gossip.

The Belfast Theater was a beautiful modern building, constructed in brick and mortar with two sets of double doors at its main entrance—one for box holders and one for the floor crowd. The grand foyer, done in Grecian style archways, led to an audience with rows of seating covered in deep green, matching the velvet curtains on the stage. The cast and crew were sitting in the audience, while Mr. Davis was on the stage with two gentlemen at his side.

"Oh good, we're all here," a voice travelled from the

front row to the aisle seat Adelia had just dropped into next to Renata. She recognized Marco Lister, a fellow actor with a goatee and a bad attitude. "I guess some of us were kept busy last night."

She felt her face flame at the innuendo and the leering chuckles from those seated around Marco.

"Someone sounds jealous," Bertie called from the row just behind Adelia. "What's wrong Marco, no one to interrupt your sleep?"

At the sound of laughter at his expense, Marco scowled but knew better than to engage with a superior adversary. Adelia turned in her seat to give Bertie a grateful smile. He winked at her just as Mr. Davis began to speak.

"Good morning all. Before we begin the run-through, I wanted to introduce you to our benefactors, Mr. Clive Morrissey and his son Mr. James Morrissey, the owners of this fine establishment. They're here this morning to invite all the actors to a soiree this evening. I've been told that there may even be some prominent Irish citizens in attendance."

Most of the actors let out exclamations of excitement and most of the crew grumbled at being left out. Adelia looked at the evening for what it was; an opportunity to look for information that might give them a lead.

Mr. Davis gestured toward stage right and another gentleman emerged from the wing, this one in his mid to late twenties with wavy blond hair. Adelia noted that several women straightened in their seats for a better view.

"As well, we have the extreme good fortune of working with Belfast's own Calen O'Donnell, our Ferdinand."

Mr. O'Donnell smiled, showing off dimples, and

waved at the audience.

"That's your leading man?" Renata whispered. "Lucky you."

After the announcements, the actors gathered backstage, preparing for a run-through. The crew had already completed a rudimentary set and would likely work long into the night to get everything ready for their dress rehearsal tomorrow.

The first act with the storm always went by quickly.

"All set, Dee?" Bertie asked, fixing the belt on his costume. He was playing Stephano—the king's drunk butler—and Adelia had never known him to be so pleased with a role.

Adelia smiled at the nickname and nodded. "As always."

"Don't think I've forgotten that you promised me a conversation about that gentleman friend of yours."

"There's really nothing to tell," Adelia said.

Bertie narrowed his eyes but fortunately he was called for a fitting and Adelia was saved once more from his interrogation.

She made it through the first act where the ship washed up on shore and Miranda met Ferdinand, her love interest. Calen did an admirable job in the part. During the second act, she wasn't needed on stage so she went with Beulah to do some measurements for petticoats. She wished Millie could have traveled with the company, but the bulk of her costuming had already been completed and Millie was due a break.

Since she was between acts, Adelia didn't have time to fully change. Fortunately Buelah was able to slip the petticoats over her day dress to take the measurements. Adelia stood perfectly still, reviewing her own performance and wondering if she'd projected adequately, when she felt the tingling in her temple.

Not now, she thought to herself.

"Miss, are you all right?"

Adelia realized she'd raised a hand to her forehead. "A bit of a headache, I think."

"I'll get you some water," Beulah hurried off. Adelia stepped down from the platform just as her vision blurred. She couldn't afford to be caught here, out in the open backstage. She saw a nearby door and fumbled to open it, making it inside just as the vision overtook her.

It was a clear night for once, she thought, looking out at the sea view through the French doors. It was the perfect night to make a trip across the channel. Soon they'd get word about the cargo. Soon their future would be set.

"Lovely evening, isn't it?"

As she turned to her companion, she caught sight of her hand. Not her hand, a man's hand.

The man speaking to her had a bald head, thick mustache and beady eyes.

"We should have heard by now."

"Be patient," the bald man said. "I have faith in our source."

Hurried footsteps came in their direction and a footman stopped in front of them, his Adam's apple bobbing in his throat as he bowed.

"I was directed to bring you this note immediately, Sir."

This was what they'd been waiting for. Dismissing the footman, she opened the note.

Shipment wilted. Please advise on next course of action.

A blinding rage took over her body and she held the note out to the mustached man.

"We still have the last shipment. We'll make do…"

The images dissolved into darkness and Adelia remembered she'd run into a storage closet with no source of light. She took deep breaths until she was sure the episode had passed. She opened the door a crack and stepped out when she saw there was no one around.

"Adelia?"

She was closing the door behind her when Renata came around the corner. She stopped and looked Adelia over. "Are you all right?"

"Yes, quite." Adelia hoped her words matched her face. "I just needed a little bit of quiet to remember my lines."

"I suppose a closet is quiet," Renata said, her brow furrowed. "Would you like to run lines with me?"

"Yes, that's very nice of you," Adelia said. "I'll just go change."

As she hurried away from Renata, Adelia couldn't help but think back on what she'd seen in her vision. Would she remember that view if she saw it again? And how would she ever explain herself to Fletcher if she started getting clues from her visions? And who was that bald man?

Fletcher was well and truly foxed.

Though, in his defense it wasn't all his doing. He'd spent the better part of the previous evening and the current afternoon in and out of the seediest pubs in Belfast. He'd thought he'd been doing his best to moderate his drinking, but as he walked down the street, the lampposts began to blur and double.

"Bloody hell," he muttered to himself. At least he'd gotten something of a lead for all his troubles.

One of the men he'd met at the pub last night had directed him to a man named Ned who spent his time gambling at the Red Rose Inn. Fletcher had spent his afternoon at the inn, drinking with the man until he could get him talking about a seaside resort where he'd worked the past summer.

The resort was near a race track and there was a port known for its lack of customs agents.

The cost of the information had been several rounds of poor quality whiskey.

At least Fletcher could console himself with the fact that Ned had gone home in worse condition and likely wouldn't remember much of his conversation with the drunk Englishman.

As he reached the hotel, Fletcher found he couldn't remember much of the walk. He stumbled up the stairs and through the door of the suite and nearly knocked Myles over.

"There you are, my lord," Myles said, straightening his jacket where Fletcher had barrelled into him. "I had wondered when to expect you home."

Fletcher looked around, taking in the dim lights in the suite's drawing room. "Did I miss supper?"

"Miss Dumont dined out," Myles said. "But she did leave a note for you."

Fletcher fell onto the nearest settee. The walk had helped clear his head enough that he was no longer seeing double. He took Adelia's note from Myles and read it over.

We've been invited to a soiree this evening at the Belfast Embassy. If your schedule allows, perhaps I will see you there -A

Fletcher could feel the first pangs of a headache in his temples.

"Shall I send for a supper tray?" Myles asked.

"Coffee," Fletcher said. "Send for coffee."

Myles prepared his evening clothes while Fletcher drank his way through the pot of black coffee that had been sent up by the kitchens. He also forced down a slice of toast, hoping it would help soak up some of the whiskey.

Dressed in navy evening clothes, he gave himself a once over in the mirror. While he wasn't fully sober, he was passable. He'd certainly gone out drunker.

"Will you require a cab?" Myles asked.

Fletcher had a fair idea which direction the Embassy was. He would have preferred to sit, but wasn't sure if he could handle the rocking motion of the carriage. Not to mention the smell of horses.

"I'll walk."

Belfast in the evening was much like London, except the drunks had better pitch when they hung out the doors of the pubs singing. As Fletcher got closer to the Embassy, the atmosphere around him shifted. Gone were the drunken revelers and shoddy inns, replaced by clean swept streets and tall houses. The genteel poverty that clung to London was absent here. The upper classes hadn't taken a financial hit the way so much of England's aristocracy had. But then, they hadn't been forced to fund a war effort.

He came upon the Embassy and noted the domed roof. It was an architectural wonder. There wasn't a line of carriages out front, which meant he was well and truly late. He hoped his arrival wouldn't cause too much of a stir.

Though some attention was always inevitable.

Fletcher walked up the steps, gave his name to a footman and was shown inside to the ballroom.

The first thing that caught his attention was the ceiling. In this room they were directly under the dome. An artist had depicted a scene out of celtic mythology, more specifically the story of *Bran mac Febail*, a man who went on a quest to the Otherworld. The images on the ceiling were of him waking to find a silver tree. Having read the mythology, Fletcher would have liked to study the mural, but in his current state, he couldn't handle staring upwards for long.

The rest of the ballroom was green and gold opulence and while it wasn't overly full, not by *ton* standards, there was quite a crowd. Fletcher made his way around the edge of the dancefloor where a waltz was in full swing. The music was just loud enough to cause his headache to return. So far there was no sign of Adelia, but he was sure she was somewhere in the crowd. Probably surrounded by a group of admirers.

"Lord Fletcher!" He heard his name called and turned

to see Mr. Davis pushing toward him through the crowd. There was a gentleman at his elbow. Of course he wanted to make an introduction. "Just the man I wanted to see this evening."

"Davis," Fletcher nodded. They were near a table laid out with jellied eel and his stomach turned over.

"May I introduce our benefactor? You met his son, James, yesterday. This is Mr. Morrissey, the senior."

The portly man bowed and Fletcher did his best to nod in return. "A pleasure to meet you, my Lord. I hear you have quite a strong textile operation going in the north."

Fletcher rarely had an opportunity to talk about his family's investments. It was considered bad manners in most drawing rooms. He would have liked nothing more than to engage in a meaningful conversation about business but the scent of jellied eel was making it impossible to focus on anything else.

"Indeed, and perhaps we can discuss it at another time? There's a certain lady I promised to meet up with." Fletcher said with what he hoped was a rakish smile and not a nauseated grimace.

"Of course," Mr. Morrissey agreed. "Perhaps you'd agree to be our guest opening night?"

"I will see you then," Fletcher said, turning toward the nearest set of French doors before anyone else could accost him. As soon as the night air hit his face his nausea dissipated and he took several deep breaths, clearing his head.

He heard a husky male voice, just around the corner, and realized he wasn't alone. From the sounds of it, the gentleman was trying to convince a lady to take a walk in the gardens with him.

Fletcher was about to head back inside to give the couple some privacy when he heard the woman's voice and stopped cold.

"I really must return," she said, her tone low, but insistent.

"There's nothing in there for you," the man continued. "Come along with me and I assure you I'll make it worth your while."

Forcing down the sudden surge of rage, Fletcher crossed the terrace and rounded the corner where the couple were mostly obscured by potted lemon trees. He found Adelia doing her best to move away from her ardent pursuer, the wall behind making progress difficult.

Though the gentleman was back on, Fletcher recognized Mr. Morrissey the younger from their brief meeting in the hotel drawing room.

"Mr. Morrissey, I really must—"

"I told you to call me James," the man said, blatantly ignoring her attempts to get away.

Fletcher forced down the instinct to punch the man in the face, particularly as he observed one of his hands holding Adelia by the shoulder. He forced a deep breath in and out. Violence was never his first response. There was no need to change tactics now.

"Adelia darling, I've been looking all over for you," Fletcher drawled. It took all his energy to force a lightness into his voice when what he really wanted was to haul James away from Adelia and toss him down the stairs.

At his words, James took a step back.

"Lord Fletcher! I hadn't heard you there."

"So I see."

"I came out for some air," Adelia said, her tone even,

though Fletcher saw the relief in her eyes as she looked in his direction. Her situation must be dire indeed if she was happy to see him.

James gave her a bow. "Thank you for accompanying me outside. Perhaps I can have the pleasure of a dance later."

Adelia gave him a curt nod but didn't answer. Fletcher waited until they were alone, watching James retreat into the ballroom, before he turned his attention back to Adelia.

"Are you all right?"

She'd opened her fan, though the air outside was cool. Fletcher noticed that she was once again wearing her signature red, though this time it was a deep, burgundy shade.

"I'm perfectly fine," she said, waving the fan in front of her face. "I've dealt with men like Mr. Morrissey all my life."

"I know you have," Fletcher said. He had first hand experience with her brand of rejection. At least he hadn't cornered her. A simple 'no' had sufficed in Fletcher's case. He held an arm out. "May I escort you back inside?"

As she stepped forward, Adelia wrinkled her nose. "What have you been drinking?"

"We can talk about it later, when my head isn't quite so bad."

She pursed her lips. "Is that why you were late? You were getting foxed?"

"I was conducting research for our case."

"You have an interesting work ethic, my lord."

Before he could explain, she swept past him, into the ballroom.

CHAPTER TEN

Adelia eyed herself in the mirror the next morning. She'd had Lilah pull her hair into a sleek knot. Upon reflection, she thought it gave her a severe look but she couldn't really be bothered to change it. Besides, it matched her mood.

"Shall I have a tray brought up?" Lilah asked.

"No need," Adelia said, reaching for her reticule. "I'll have breakfast in the dining room."

Watching people was one of Adelia's favorite activities, and with travellers coming from all over, a hotel was one of the most interesting places to observe others.

She also hoped it would help to calm her nerves. Today was their dress rehearsal followed by opening night, and she needed to have her head on straight.

Adelia walked out into the shared drawing room and stopped short.

There, seated on a settee with the morning newspaper was a very awake and alert Lord Fletcher.

"What are you doing up?"

"And a very good morning to you as well," Fletcher said with a nod. "Shall I call for a breakfast tray?"

"I'm going to the dining room."

"Then I'll join you there," Fletcher said, getting to his feet.

Adelia searched her brain for a reason to go alone, but couldn't find one. Finally, she found her voice as he held open the door of the suite for her.

"I didn't expect you to be up this early."

"My dear, I don't believe we've spent nearly enough time together for you to say with any certainty what my usual hours are. Now, would you like to stand in the doorway of our suite? Or shall we go down to breakfast?"

Not wanting to risk anyone wandering past and listening in on their conversation, Adelia walked out into the hallway and headed for the staircase. Fletcher caught up with her and was at her side as she stepped into the grand foyer. She allowed him to lead her to the dining room where he requested a table in a quiet corner. They were seated against the far wall, surrounded by empty tables.

Had she been on her own, Adelia would have wanted a better view of the room, but knowing Fletcher would draw attention wherever he went, she was grateful for the space between herself and the other diners.

"Am I to assume that having breakfast together is part of the plan to solidify your appearance here in Belfast as my companion?"

Fletcher picked up his menu and flipped it over. "Not at all. That's behind us."

"Then why are we here?"

Adelia hadn't picked up her menu—she already knew what she wanted. Instead, she watched Fletcher as he perused the items. He looked different this morning. Sober. Both in mind and body.

"Because we need to discuss our mission."

Adelia straightened in her chair. "You've remembered that then have you?"

The waiter returned at that moment, leaving a coffee tray and taking their food order.

Fletcher poured two cups of coffee, pushing one toward her side of the table. "I've been gathering information."

Adelia added a touch of cream to her coffee. She noted that Fletcher dropped no less than four cubes of sugar into his.

"From where? A distillery?"

"Close, actually. I had to visit a number of pubs."

"Had to?"

Fletcher quirked an eyebrow. The gesture was equal parts endearing and annoying.

"I have to go where the investigation takes me."

"And what have you learned from your trip to the pub?"

Fletcher didn't immediately answer. The waiter returned with two covered dishes and set them down. She watched as Fletcher uncovered his plate of sausages while she picked up the jam jar placing a dollop on her scone. She'd never been much of one for breakfast, but she always had tea or coffee in the mornings and she knew from the tray she'd had the previous morning that the scones were exceptional.

Though, she found herself pondering Fletcher's actions from the previous day rather than eating.

"I think I've got a lead," Fletcher said. "A place where the ladies might be being held. Or, at least where they were held."

"You've figured it out already?"

Fletcher's lips twitched and he very nearly smiled at her. Adelia realized that while he almost always wore an amused expression, he rarely smiled. She wondered what it would take to change that. Then she wondered why she would care.

Adelia gave herself a mental shake and picked up her scone while Fletcher continued talking.

"There are a couple of resort towns, not too far away. I should be able to make it there and back in a day or two at the most."

Adelia frowned. "Is that safe?"

"If it wasn't, I wouldn't go." Fletcher cut into his sausage. "But I did want you to be aware that it might be necessary for me to leave town for a bit. Don't worry, you'll be safe."

"It isn't my safety I'm worried about. I thought it wasn't advisable for agents to go on missions alone."

"It isn't, but since I made that rule I think I can be the one to break it."

"That isn't amusing."

"I assure you, I wasn't intending to be."

Adelia wasn't sure why it bothered her that Fletcher might go out on his own. It wasn't like she could stop him anyway. Perhaps it was because if it were Meri she wouldn't have let him go alone.

It didn't feel right to let your partner go without you. Even if that partner was Lord Fletcher. Besides, after the vision she'd had at her rehearsal, she felt like she was in a position to identify the location. Though, that wasn't something she could share.

"Perhaps you should wait until we can go together."

Fletcher shook his head. "There's no time. We only have a fortnight and you don't have a day off for what? A week?"

"Yes."

"It makes more sense for me to go ahead, see if there's anything worthwhile and if there is we can talk about a plan going forward."

It wasn't an ideal situation, but Adelia couldn't see a way around it. "When will you leave?"

"In a day or so, depending on how long it takes to get a carriage together."

Adelia glanced at the large clock on the wall of the dining room. "I should get to rehearsal."

"All ready for opening night then?"

"As ready as we can be," Adelia agreed.

"Would you like me to walk you to the theater?"

"Of course not," Adelia said, then realized how sharp her tone was. "You still have breakfast to finish and I'm well capable of getting there on my own."

Fletcher tilted his head as he looked at her and for a moment Adelia thought he was about to argue, but instead he gave her a nod. "I'll see you this evening then."

Adelia had to hurry to make it to the theater in time and given she was running behind schedule, she wasn't surprised that she didn't see any members of the company along the way. Once inside the Belfast Theater she went to the stage door where Beulah was waiting to get her into her first costume.

"It would happen that the one time I'm late we start on time," Adelia said as she rushed out of the dressing area, Beulah on her heels, fussing with Adelia's hair as they went.

Adelia stopped backstage next to Bertie, waiting for her cue.

"Slow down, you made it with time to spare," he said, giving her a quick once over. "Would it be indiscrete of me to ask what kept you this morning?"

"I'm sure you'll ask anyway," Adelia said.

"I know you, Dee. You don't have affairs."

Adelia raised an eyebrow. "What about Captain Lancaster?"

"I know for a fact you and Captain Lancaster were friends, which makes this whole situation with Lord Fletcher all the more intriguing."

"What are you trying to say Bertie?"

"Only that I don't want you getting your heart broken. We both know that men of his class think of people like us."

I could never care for someone like you.

Fletcher's words from her vision echoed through her head unbidden.

Fortunately, Adelia was saved from having to answer Bertie as a trio of actresses walked by. Renata, dressed in blues for her part as the Greek goddess of sea and sky, paused to speak to Adelia, eyeing the dress Millie had so painstakingly repaired.

"Your costume is lovely. I swear this part was written for you."

"Leaving aside the fact the play was written over two hundred years ago," Bertie muttered. Adelia gave him a poke in the side before turning a smile on Renata.

"It's kind of you to say so. I'm sure you'll get your chance at a lead role soon."

Renata beamed and hurried off with the other goddesses.

"Be careful around her," Bertie said, his eyes on the retreating actresses. The ladies had their sights set on Calen O'Donnell and Adelia couldn't blame them. In her limited interactions the Irish actor had been nothing but charming.

"You're filled with warnings today. It's no fun. Besides, it's unwarranted. Renata is a sweet girl and she looks up to me."

"She doesn't look up to you, she wants to be you."

Adelia rolled her eyes, but as she was about to go on stage, she didn't bother to argue.

"The resort is near the sea, ain't it? But hardly anyone goes there."

Fletcher was seated across from yet another informant in yet another grubby pub. This time he'd at least had the good sense to water down his whiskey.

The man across from him had not bothered. Rudy—as he was known—was on his sixth drink since Fletcher had joined him. Tired of refilling glasses, the bartender had left a bottle in the middle of the table.

He'd told Adelia that he had a fair idea where to start, but the truth was there were several resorts near the race track. He had to double check he was going to the correct one. He appreciated that she wanted to help, but between dress rehearsals yesterday and preparations for opening night tonight, she'd been far too busy. Besides, that was her job, keeping the attention off him while he wandered in and out of seedy inns. No one cared what a drunk English man was up to when the great Adelia Dumont was in town.

"This resort—is it open to the public?" Fletcher asked.

Rudy rubbed his bulbous nose off the back of his wrist. "That's the thing, it is but it isn't."

Fletcher checked his watch. The curtain rose on opening night in half an hour. He really needed to wrap up this meeting.

"You say I could make the journey there in a day?"

Rudy nodded. "It's called Briarwood."

"It's near the race track?"

"Aye."

Fletcher set a few coins down on the table. "Thanks for your time. Have a round on me."

"Don't mind if I do," Rudy belched as he pawed at the coins. Fletcher pulled the brim of his hat down as he exited the tavern and headed toward the theater. He should be able to make it with a few minutes to spare.

As he walked, the dwellings around him slowly changed from rundown boarding houses to modest townhomes to well kept mansions. Rounding the corner to the Belfast Theater, he could already see the line of patrons waiting to get in. Since he had reserved a box, Fletcher could have gone to the second entrance, but he'd made good time on his walk and was in no hurry. He settled in behind a working class couple as the line began to move.

"I heard the Queen herself goes to see her performances. Sometimes twice a week," a woman with red curls said to her companion, a man with dark hair and eyes.

"If she's even half the looker that they say she is, it'll be worth the price of admission," the man said.

"And I heard the line of admirers outside her dressing room door goes right around backstage," the woman continued.

Fletcher smiled to himself. Indeed, Adelia was doing her job just by being in town.

The line moved quickly, and soon Fletcher was near enough to the front that he broke off and presented his ticket at a second entrance where the usher let him go up to the box level. Realizing who his companions were for the evening, he was somewhat relieved to have arrived close to curtain call.

"Lord Fletcher!" Mr. Davis beamed as he greeted him. There were three other guests as well, including Mr. Clive Morrissey, a woman he assumed was his wife, and their son, James. "I worried you wouldn't make it in time."

"Got caught up in the crowd," Fletcher said, taking in the other occupants of the box, his eyes narrowing in on James Morrissey.

"My lord," Morrissey senior stepped forward. "May I present my wife? Mrs. Lydia Morrissey."

"A pleasure," Fletcher took the lady's gloved hand. While Mr. Morrissey was portly and slightly balding, Mrs.

Morrissey retained a youthful appearance.

A bell sounded and Fletcher took the seat next to Mrs. Morrissey, grateful that he could avoid the son. He wasn't quite ready to deal with him yet, not when he could still so easily picture the man's hands all over Adelia.

Mrs. Morrissey was a pleasant, though somewhat vapid lady. Fortunately Fletcher didn't have to make conversation for long as the curtain went up almost as soon as he took his seat.

The opening scene was a storm at sea. Fletcher had seen *The Tempest* numerous times, but had to admit that Davis' crew had done a superlative job using sound and a tilting floor to mimic gale force winds.

But as impressive as the storm was, it was nothing compared to Adelia's appearance on stage as Miranda. For a moment Fletcher was completely taken in by her performance. The lonely young woman, living on an island with her father. There was something almost magical about her first encounter with a man near her own age.

It wasn't until the curtain came down at intermission that Fletcher remembered where he was and who he was with.

It had been like this the first time he'd seen her. She'd just finished playing Ophelia in *Hamlet*, and while Fletcher hadn't been impressed by the lead actor, he had gone to see the show twice. Then he'd gone backstage to meet the main actress and things had gone terribly sideways.

"Lord Fletcher!"

He looked up to see that James was standing just behind him with another man at his side. At some point Mrs. Morrissey had gotten up and he hadn't even noticed.

"This is my friend, Walter Jackson," James pointed at the bald mustached man to his right. "He's in shipping."

If they don't stop introducing me to people, I'm going to have to keep a notebook for names, Fletcher thought to himself.

"Ah, I have a few friends in shipping myself," Fletcher said.

"Well, I'd be happy to be added to the number," Jackson said. There was something calculating in the man's eyes, as though he saw ledgers instead of people.

"Are you gentlemen enjoying the show?" Fletcher asked.

"We are," James agreed. "Though probably not as much as you."

"Yes, I heard you came here with the actress," Jackson said, his lips pulling into a smirk. "Leave it to the English to beat us to the treasure even before it arrives on shore."

James laughed and Fletcher forced his face to remain neutral. What he really wanted was to poke the bald man between his beady eyes.

Fortunately, the play started again.

Fletcher allowed himself to be swept up into the second half, though not as completely as the first. This time he couldn't help glancing over his shoulder to watch how James and Jackson were eyeing Adelia. They'd even exchanged whispers and smug smiles a few times. Fletcher fought off the uncomfortable urge to hit someone.

When the curtain dropped, he waited and went backstage with Mr. Davis and the other members of their box. The green room at the theater wasn't quite as large as the one in London, but it was well-appointed and the drinks were flowing. Interestingly enough, it was also decorated in shades of green.

Fletcher immediately went in search of a brandy, hoping to get a moment to himself, but Jackson and James stayed glued to his side.

The actors slowly trickled in and for a moment Fletcher thought a pretty young woman who'd played one of the Roman goddesses had caught Walter's eye, but the man stayed at his side.

"There she is," James said as Adelia arrived on the arm of Bertie. She wore a gown of cherry red that drew the eye of everyone in the room—male and female.

She looked around with her usual polite smile in place, but her gaze froze when she landed on Fletcher. No, he realized after a moment. Not him. His companion. She was watching Jackson.

For a moment her gaze faltered and her smile slipped, but then she righted herself. Fletcher went to her side, offering her his arm. Once she was away from Bertie, she looked from him to Jackson.

"How do you know that man?" she asked, dropping her voice.

"James introduced me. His taste in friends appears to be as questionable as his manners. Why?"

"I don't have a good feeling about him." Though they were in the midst of a serious conversation, Adelia kept her smile in place and nodded at the other actors as they passed. "What does he do?"

"Shipping, I believe. I can ask Duncan about him when we are back in London."

"I think you should stay away from him," Adelia

said.

Fletcher wanted to ask where her concern came from, but they were interrupted by Davis who insisted on taking Adelia around the room to receive the congratulations of everyone present. He'd have to ask her about her strange feeling about Jackson later.

CHAPTER ELEVEN

Adelia had the morning off. That was the upside to a good opening night, it meant that she didn't need to go in for early rehearsals. And after the previous evening, she was grateful to have some time to think.

"What shall we do, Miss?" Lilah asked. "Perhaps some shopping?"

Not normally one for wandering in and out of stores, Adelia had to admit the idea of walking through the streets without having to worry about a mask was most appealing.

They set off on foot and soon found themselves on a street lined with dressmakers, milliners, a general store and a bookshop. They spent the better part of an hour looking over ribbons because Lilah wanted to re-trim Adelia's bonnets. It wasn't Adelia's favorite way to pass the time, but Lilah loved fashion and clothes and her enthusiasm had been contagious. Lilah was in the process of picking out ribbon to add to her collection when the bell over the door rang and Myles entered. He immediately came over to bid them good morning and Adelia noted the blush in Lilah's cheeks.

"What brings you here this morning?" Adelia asked.

"A shocking lack of handkerchiefs," Myles said with a grin. "Have you ladies been here long?"

"I was just leaving," Adelia said before Lilah could speak. "I need to check out the bookshop next door. But perhaps you wouldn't mind keeping Lilah company while she finishes her shopping?"

Lilah gave her a wide eyed look, but Adelia ignored it, focusing on Myles instead. He gave her a grin.

"It would be my pleasure, Miss."

Adelia smiled to herself as she left the store. The bookshop was only two doors down and as soon as she stepped inside she was overcome by the dusty smell of paper. The scent filled her with childhood memories. Mostly happy, though also sad. She pushed those aside and wandered further into the shop.

She'd been fortunate to spend her early childhood in a bookstore owned by her father and uncle. It had been there that she'd learned to read and write and in some ways it was also where she'd learned her passion for acting, memorizing passages out of books and reciting them to the regular customers.

Then, of course, everything had gone horribly wrong.

Movement outside the storefront window caught her eye and Adelia saw two men walking past—James Morrissey and the bald man—Mr. Jackson. A cold shiver ran down her spine and she backed away from the window. She wasn't certain, but she thought they were coming toward the shop. She headed back, hiding between the stacks of books.

Adelia hadn't gotten an opportunity to talk to Fletcher

about Mr. Jackson as they'd both been exhausted when they'd arrived back at the suite. Upon further reflection, she wasn't even really certain what she could say to Fletcher anyway. She couldn't tell him she'd seen him in a vision. He'd think she'd lost her mind.

Even she wasn't certain that she hadn't.

She'd pushed her visions out of her head, intending to deal with them after opening night, but upon seeing Mr. Jackson, she couldn't put it off any longer.

Adelia had a bad feeling about him.

She waited in the back of the store, but heard no one enter the shop. Letting out a breath she looked at the shelves around her. Poetry.

Her father had always said reading poetry was like solving riddles, trying to figure out exactly what sentiment the writer was looking to convey. She reached up and was about to pull a volume of Tennyson off a shelf when she felt the tingling in her forehead.

Not here, she thought to herself, but the vision was swift, already overtaking her.

She sat in a smoke-filled room, at a table laid out with chips and cards. Her companions were losing badly, but she didn't care.

Or, more accurately, this man whose eyes she saw through didn't care.

He turned to the bald gentleman at his side. There sat Mr. Walter Jackson.

"What did you think of the play?" He asked.

Jackson dropped his cards and pulled on his mustache. "I don't care for pretty words, but the scenery was nice enough. The lead actress was something to behold. I'd like to get her on her own, away from her companion."

"Oh, I think that could be arranged."

"Indeed?" Jackson pulled on his mustache. "I'd be in your debt."

"More so than you already are, you mean?"

The vision faded and the gaming room dissolved around her, leaving her once again in the bookshop, gripping the edge of a shelf, while a set of deep hazel eyes watched her intently from only a few feet away.

Handkerchiefs. Fletcher had been dragged out of bed with the most meager of breakfasts all so Myles could fetch him more handkerchiefs.

"It's not as though you have anything else to do this morning, my lord," Myles said as they'd entered a street lined in shops. "And you had said you wanted to start rising earlier."

Fletcher grunted. His valet wasn't wrong, but he wasn't fully prepared to admit that yet.

"I'll pop into the general store, shall I?" Myles said. "And see what they've got."

"Go ahead," Fletcher agreed. "Nothing too fussy and pick up some for yourself as well."

"Yes, my lord."

With Myles off, Fletcher wandered the street on his own intending to get a proper meal. He passed a giggling group of ladies surrounding a lone gentleman and realized they were from the theater company—Fletcher was fairly certain the man had played opposite Adelia the night before. He saw them heading to the tea shop and decided his own stomach could wait. He stepped into a pewter shop instead and placed an order for a monogrammed serving set to be sent back to London for Duncan and Hazel's wedding. He was sure his mother would pick something out, but Fletcher wanted to send his own gift to his friends.

He went back outside and stopped in his tracks. If he wasn't very much mistaken, James Morrissey and Walter Jackson were heading down the street just ahead of him. The last thing he wanted was to get caught up in conversation with either gentleman again this morning. He noticed that they passed by the bookshop and Fletcher saw his opportunity.

He slipped inside and nodded to the shopkeeper, an elderly man who squinted over a book on the counter. Fletcher wasn't sure the man had actually seen him, but he continued inside, navigating through the shelves of books.

As a child and even young man he'd been a great reader. Especially novels and adventure stories. But once his father had passed on, there hadn't been as much time for frivolity. His reading included newspapers and reports from other agents, as well as the letters from his chief steward who looked after the main holdings in the north, but he still made time for novels.

Fletcher paused, taking Sir Garrett Jones' most recent publication off the shelf. He opened the cover, reading the first few lines, and decided to buy it. Between shopping for a wedding gift and now a novel, he wasn't sure when he'd last had such an idle morning.

There was a shuffling sound in the next row of shelves

and Fletcher thought he heard someone gasp. He rounded into the next aisle and came to a stop. There, frozen in place just in front of him was Adelia.

He knew what was happening, though he hadn't seen an episode quite like this before. Still, he was familiar enough with the aether fever to know when someone was suffering an attack.

As he watched, she moved her lips, though no sound came out. She was completely unaware of his presence. Or of anything else for that matter.

He kept a lookout, but fortunately no one else came into the store and the shopkeeper was taken in with his own reading. Lost in the vision, Fletcher knew she was completely unaware of her surroundings. Her brandy colored eyes gazed through him. He noted that a few golden strands of hair had fallen loose from their pins. She was wearing pink again, this time a deep rose. She wore the color often, but it suited her, giving her complexion a soft glow.

Normally, Adelia had her society mask on. Her polite, though slightly removed smile she wore when not on stage. But in this moment her guard was down. She looked young; her face held a naked beauty that he'd never seen on stage.

He was staring.

She blinked and he realized she must be coming around. When she saw him standing in the aisle, her eyes grew round. When she spoke her voice was rough.

"What are you doing here?"

Fletcher held up the book in his hand. "Shopping."

She took a step back and he noticed that her hands

were shaking. He needed to act fast before she withdrew from him completely.

"There's a tea shop across the street," he said. "Let me escort you."

He thought she was going to argue, but instead she nodded. "Give me a minute. Go take care of your purchase."

It went against his instincts to leave her alone, but there was no way she could exit the shop without his notice.

He went up to the shopkeeper, who looked up from his book, surprised that there was a customer in his shop. Adelia appeared just as Fletcher was being handed his purchase, now wrapped in brown paper with a string.

"Shall we?" Fletcher held his arm out and she took it, leaving the shop with him. Still a little pale, Adelia appeared to have regained her composure as they crossed the street. Her mask was firmly back in place.

Though, the hand resting on his arm held on with slightly more pressure than usual, as though she needed the support. No matter how put together she appeared, Adelia hadn't fully recovered from her episode.

Inside the tea shop, the other young actors had taken up a large table near the front. They called and waved at Adelia, but while she nodded back, she didn't pause to talk, instead letting Fletcher lead her to a corner table.

"Tea and scones," Fletcher said to the waiter as they were seated. "With jam."

When the waiter left them, Fletcher looked at Adelia, waiting for her to speak. She pulled at the thumb of her left glove.

"Thank you for your assistance in the bookshop, I'm

afraid I was slightly indisposed. I felt a headache coming on—"

"I know it's the fever," Fletcher cut her off.

Her brown eyes grew hard, but Fletcher didn't care. Her lies bothered him more than her affliction. "I don't know what you're talking about."

"We don't have time for stories. You need to be upfront with me or you could be in grave danger."

"I'm not in danger here," Adelia said. "Everyone thinks I'm an actress not an agent."

"That's not what I mean. Women like you are going missing."

"Women like me?" Adelia repeated.

The waiter returned with a tray and Fletcher didn't wait for him to pour. He reached for the teapot and a cup, dismissing the waiter. Adelia pulled off her gloves as Fletcher handed her a cup of tea.

"What I mean is, the women who have gone missing all suffer from the fever."

Adelia held her cup between her hands, but didn't drink from it. "I did assume as much, given they were taken from Cravenwood."

"What do you think motivated their kidnappers?"

"A ransom, since some are from very good families. What other reason could people have for abducting women with an illness?"

"What if the illness came with certain abilities?"

Adelia grew perfectly still, staring into her tea. "What sort of abilities?"

Fletcher paused, resting his cup back on its saucer. He knew he needed to proceed with caution if he didn't want to spook her.

"I know about the visions."

She drew her lips into a thin line and looked up, finally meeting his gaze. "Are you going to use this information to have me thrown out of the Agency?"

Fletcher leaned back as though she'd actually struck him. "You think I'd do that?"

"I know the fever makes people nervous. I'm not stupid."

"I never said you were."

"So what then? You'll keep my secret?"

"I will."

She eased back into her chair, even brought her cup to her lips. "I'm on an excellent treatment plan. It won't ever interfere with my work."

"Could it possibly enhance it though?"

Adelia put down her cup with a clang, spilling a few drops of tea onto the saucer.

"I'm sure I don't know what you are talking about."

"Then let me enlighten you." Fletcher leaned forward, pushing the plate of scones towards Adelia's side of the table. "But while I do that, you must eat."

She picked up a scone, setting it on her plate and looked to him to continue but Fletcher refused to speak until, with much grumbling, she dropped a dollop of jam onto her plate and finally took a bite.

Fletcher watched her eat and formulated the words he'd use in his head. It was important to him that he keep the identity of the woman he was about to talk about a secret, not only as a professional courtesy, but also because he considered her a friend.

"I heard a story recently about a woman whose aether induced visions turned out to be a reality. In fact, they led us towards solving a case."

Adelia swallowed hard. Fletcher wasn't certain he'd be able to convince her to eat another bite.

"You believe that's possible?" she asked.

"I didn't, not immediately, but I do now."

"What changed your mind?"

"Amongst other things, a cargo bay filled with women whose only commonality was the fever. I believe the women were being kidnapped because someone knew about their extraordinary abilities and was trying to weaponize them."

She stared at him, biting her lower lip as though afraid to speak. Fletcher reached across the table, resting his fingers on her gloved hand.

"Whatever else you believe, you must know that if you choose to share the information from your visions with me, I will keep the source a secret."

CHAPTER TWELVE

He knew.

Adelia's hand shook as she powdered her face. She'd been lost in thought while her hair and make-up were applied. The conversations she'd had with Fletcher played over and over in her mind.

Not only did he know about her visions, but he believed they were real.

Fletcher had a meeting that evening to prepare for his trip out of town. She suspected if he hadn't had an appointment to get to he would have stayed at the tea shop all day asking her about her visions. She'd told him about Mr. Jackson's presence and between them they'd tried to reason out what she'd seen. He'd had a lot of questions about what was said and what she saw. They'd stayed in the tea shop for hours.

"Who do you suppose Jackson was speaking to?" Fletcher asked after she'd described the second vision.

"I think it was the same person both times," Adelia said. She'd hesitated over her most recent theory, but then had decided she had nothing to lose. "I think it's James Morrissey."

Fletcher had straightened up his chair. "Why do you suspect him?"

"It's more of an idea I've had about how the visions work. I think they're linked to people who are near me when the visions happen."

"And Mr. Morrissey the younger was around both times?"

"Yes."

Fletcher had nodded slowly. "It's a good theory. Is that how it's been before, with other visions?"

Adelia thought back to the evening at the spectacle with Ronnie Lovejoy. "Yes, that's how it usually is."

When she'd returned to the hotel, she'd had a hot bath and strongly considered having a drink to calm her nerves. However, she shot the thought down. She had a performance to prepare for.

"You ready, Miss Dumont?" Renata asked. The young woman was decked out in her slightly scandalous goddess costume. Adelia was happy she no longer had to take those background roles that were more about ogling than acting.

"I am," Adelia said. And it was the truth. She was ready to push her own worries to the side and pretend to be someone else for a few hours.

"Is your lord here this evening?"

Adelia forced a smile. "He isn't. But I will see him afterwards."

Renata laughed. "He came all this way to be with you. A man has to be mad for you to chase you all the way to Belfast."

Or mad in general, Adelia thought to herself, though

she knew that wasn't the case with Fletcher. At least, not completely.

Which, she realized, was something of a revelation. He was far more substantive than she'd previously thought.

The show went off without a hitch. Opening night was always filled with nerves and minor mishaps, but by the second show they were getting into a routine. She took her bow with Calen at her side and went back to her dressing room to change and was surprised to find a vase full of pink roses on her table with a note.

Do not go to the green room until I arrive - F

Adelia dropped the note next to the vase. She found she was equal parts touched and annoyed. On the one hand, the flowers were thoughtful. On the other, she didn't like receiving orders and the fact that she wasn't to leave without him likely meant he'd be arriving late.

As much as Adelia truly loved the stage, the socializing afterwards was a chore she had to get through. Occasionally, if Meri were in town, she could get out of spending time in the green room or whatever other event had been planned. But usually she needed to make an appearance. It was expected of a lead actress in particular.

One of the dressers came by to take her costume and help her into a wine colored evening gown.

"Miss, may I ask why you always wear reds and pinks?" the dresser, a young woman of maybe eighteen, asked.

"I've been told that those are my colors," Adelia said, thinking fondly of her London dressmaker, Madam de

Meliodor. "And once I was told that, I found I couldn't feel as comfortable in anything else."

"Well, I agree with you there, Miss. It is a lovely color on you."

Adelia took a look at herself in the full length mirror. Because of the deep color, the dress had few embellishments, making it relatively comfortable, at least for an evening gown. It was cut slightly lower in the bust than she usually wore, but wasn't scandalous by any means. She turned around to pick up her gloves when she felt a tingling sensation in her temple.

"Are you all right, Miss?" the dresser asked.

"Yes, I just need my reticule."

"Here it is." The young woman held out the black satin purse.

"Thank you for your help tonight," Adeilia said, dismissing the young woman. When she was alone, she took her pillbox out and swallowed an extra blocker. She could still feel the tension in her temple, but her symptoms weren't worsening.

There was no way she was going to make it if she had to wait hours for Fletcher to return. She'd go to the green room, do a quick round, then meet Fletcher back at the hotel.

Fortunately she met Bertie in the hallway outside the dressing rooms and he offered to escort her.

"You were fabulous tonight," he said as they strolled down the hall, toward an exit that would lead them to the backstage area. "Not that you ever give a bad performance, but Miranda might be your defining role."

"You think so?" Adelia asked. She was surprised by

the assessment. Bertie was never one for false praise. "She's an interesting character—much more so than Juliet or Ophelia—but I can't see that I have all that much in common with her."

"Can't you?" Bertie paused and Adelia stopped next to him. They were now standing next to the ship's mast from the first act.

"She's young and naive," Adelia said. "And in want of a man."

Bertie laughed. "She's young, yes, and despite your efforts to cover it up, so are you. And while I can't argue that she is naive, I believe that is a mere matter of her circumstances rather than disposition."

"I will grant you that, but I don't believe I was ever so eager to meet a man as she was."

"A man? No indeed. Miranda was eager to meet her freedom. Her escape if you will."

Adelia swallowed hard. Their conversation had taken a strange turn. Bertie appeared to be in a rare philosophical mood. "But I am free."

"Are you?" His eyes assessed her. "Are you certain that, in your attempt to escape your past, you haven't closed yourself off on a brand new island?"

Adelia opened her mouth, ready to respond, but then stopped. Of course it wasn't true. Certainly she'd worked hard to get off the streets, but that didn't mean she was closed off. She wasn't an island. She had her work, both on stage and with the Agency.

"You've had only yourself to rely on for so long," he continued. "You don't have to do that forever. This is your brave new world too."

Adelia swallowed hard. She could feel the tears pricking the back of her eyes and it wasn't like her to cry. Not unless the role called for it.

"If this is about Lord Fletcher—"

Bertie cut her off. "Whatever is going on there isn't my business. At least, not unless you want it to be. You can handle yourself."

"Then why bring all this up now?"

He shrugged, a boyish grin lighting up his features. "I may not trust Lord Fletcher, but since he's been around you've been out and about more. I think it's good for you. You've been in hiding too long."

"Hardly hiding, I'm an actress."

"Yes, and it's time you left the roles on stage."

With that cryptic remark, Bertie patted her hand and they continued walking.

The gathering in the green room was in full swing when they arrived. Adelia left Bertie next to a table filled with sweets while she went to make her rounds.

The tingling in her forehead hadn't fully subsided but she only needed to put in a few minutes.

"Are you quite well, Miss Dumont?"

Adelia stopped, looking over her shoulder to find Calen O'Donnell next to her, cutting a dashing figure in his evening clothes. At his question she realized she was touching her temple and she dropped her hand.

"I am, thank you. Just a little tired."

"Indeed, given your performance I don't see how you couldn't be. Have I told you what an honor it is to act alongside you?"

"You have not, but perhaps that's because you are

usually surrounded by admirers."

Calen laughed, glancing toward the corner where the trio of young actresses were watching him. Renata waved him over.

"They are such charming ladies."

"It's hardly polite to stay away," Adelia added.

"You are correct, Miss Dumont. You are certain you are well?"

"I am. You are released."

Mr. O'Donnell grinned and moved on. Adelia turned to find Mr. Davis so she could let him know she'd made an appearance, when she was greeted by far less charming company.

"The fair Miss Dumont, how lovely you look this evening."

Her heart sank as she turned around to find James Morrissey and Mr. Jackson, both giving her assessing looks. Adelia forced a pleasant smile.

"Thank you. I didn't expect to see you again so soon."

"Indeed. Given your performance last night, I found I could not wait to return to see you again."

As Mr. Jackson's gaze rested on her chest, Adelia's stomach rolled and she was glad she hadn't eaten more than a light supper. All she could think about was her last vision and how Mr. Jackson had been talking about her, likely to the man at his side.

"Your stage abilities are second only to your stunning beauty," Mr. Jackson said, still not looking her in the eye.

Her head tingled again and she touched her fingers to her temple.

"Are you well?" Mr. Jackson looked her over, his gaze resting on her forehead.

"Yes," Adelia said, not liking the glint in his eye. Or perhaps she'd imagined it. Either way it was time to change the subject. She found most men, when given the opportunity, were keen to talk about themselves. "Tell me about your business endeavors."

Fletcher had gone to Adelia's dressing room, only to find that she hadn't paid his instructions the slightest attention. He'd spent the most tedious evening finding a carriage to rent and arrived at the theater to find that Adelia had gone off without him. Checking his temper, he headed to the backstage area and into the large room where actors and select patrons gathered after the show. Unlike the grand soirees leading up to opening night, this gathering was smaller and much more intimate.

Fletcher paused in the doorway. No one had noted his arrival as the guests and actors were mingling. There was an animated group of women around the lead actor but that wasn't where Fletcher's gaze rested. No, he was much more focused on finding Adelia.

As the room wasn't especially large, it didn't take him long to spot her. Her deep wine colored dress set off her complexion to perfection, giving her gold hair an almost bronze undertone. The garment was simple and elegant in design and, though still modest, showed more skin than he was accustomed to seeing her reveal. And he wasn't the only one to notice.

Fletcher narrowed his eyes as he watched Walter Jackson's eyes drift from her face down below her neck. The temper that he's managed to tame just a few moments ago came roaring to life. His fingers itched with the urge to drag the other man out of the room by his stupid mustache.

As he made his way towards Adelia, there was something else Fletcher noted. Something that froze him inside, cooling his temper as a sense of dread took its place. She was rubbing her temple with her fingers. Even as Fletcher noticed the gesture, Jackson's eyes moved back up Adelia's body, settling on her forehead.

Fletcher increased his speed, nearly knocking over an actress who'd played one of the goddesses, he forgot which one. He apologized and continued pushing forward, not stopping until he was at Adelia's side.

Fortunately she'd dropped her hand and was no longer drawing attention to her forehead.

"Tell me about your business endeavors." Fletcher heard her say as he settled next to her.

"So sorry to interrupt," Fletcher interjected, "but I need to borrow Miss Dumont for a moment."

Jackson chuckled, it was a grating sound that held no mirth. Fletcher wasn't surprised to see James Morrissey as well. He was starting to think Jackson had grown the other man as a shadow. Fletcher forced his face to remain neutral as Jackson gave Adelia a knowing wink.

"Better leave you to your protector," he said. "But perhaps we could continue our conversation another time?"

"Of course," Adelia answered. Her face held its usual polite smile but Fletcher could see the lines around her mouth were forced.

As the two men walked away, Fletcher didn't wait for anyone else to take their place. He took Adelia by the arm and headed across the room.

"Where are we going?" she asked as several of the other actors waved for her to join them. Fletcher ignored their invitations and continued toward the door.

"We are leaving."

"But I've only just arrived."

"From what I've seen, you've been here quite long enough."

Adelia stopped, forcing Fletcher to do the same unless he wanted to be seen dragging her from the green room.

"Are you angry?"

Fletcher very nearly choked on his words. "You have to ask?"

She raised an eyebrow. "Apparently so."

"We'll talk about it once we have some privacy."

Adelia looked around, realizing that they were standing in the middle of the green room and several sets of eyes were watching their exchange, trying to decide whether or not the couple was, in fact, arguing.

Fletcher made a snap decision, pulling Adelia to him, close enough that the side of her body was flush against him and her sweet scent filled his nostrils. He leaned in close to her ear to whisper.

"We cannot be seen to argue in public."

As his breath hit her earlobe she let out a small shiver and as he leaned back he could see that her cheeks had reddened. Anyone watching them was in no doubt as to the reason they were leaving the party and no one stopped them as they made their escape.

Adelia quietly allowed him to take the lead until they were outside the theater. Then she stopped in the middle of the sidewalk and turned on him.

"How dare you drag me out like that!"

"Like what?" Fletcher's voice rose to match hers. "Like we're lovers?"

Adelia took a step back, her cloak half open and her chest heaving. Fletcher forced his gaze back up to her face.

"We are not lovers and you know it!"

"Yes, but it would be in our best interest if all of Belfast didn't know it or else they might wonder why I'm here with you."

At the subtle reminder of their mission, Adelia appeared to calm down, at least slightly. She continued walking toward the hotel, though she held her arms away from Fletcher. He easily matched his stride to hers, neither of them speaking until they arrived in their drawing room of the suite.

They dismissed Lilah and Myles, both of whom had been waiting up, and once they were alone, Fletcher went to the side table to pour himself a brandy.

"Would you like a drink?" he offered Adelia, but she was pacing in front of the fireplace and glared instead of answering him. Fletcher took his glass and sat in one of the nearby armchairs.

Lilah and Myles had turned the gas lamps to half light and neither Fletcher nor Adelia had turned them back up. There was a low fire in the grate, but not enough to give any real illumination. As Adelia walked back and forth in front of him, shadows played over her features. Yet, he didn't need better lighting to know she was angry with him.

"You humiliated me in front of my peers," she said, finally finding her voice. "How am I supposed to face them tomorrow?"

"The same way you always do?" Fletcher said, rubbing his chin. "I don't see what the problem is. They already think we're in a relationship."

Adelia stopped and turned to face him, her skirt fanning out behind her. "The problem is I never show such... displays in public."

She was mad about their embrace? Fletcher would have laughed if the woman in front of him wasn't just about ready to breathe fire in his direction.

Then something else occurred to him. Something that filled him with a warm pleasant feeling.

"You never show any sort of affection in public?"

"Certainly not." Her nostrils flared. "I know others make assumptions about my relationships, but I never invite those sorts of interactions. It sets a bad precedent."

Fletcher couldn't fault her there. He'd seen the way men pawed at actresses and singers and women in general. He took a long sip of his brandy.

"I believe you are forgetting that all of this could have been avoided if you had simply obeyed orders."

"Orders?" Adelia crossed her arms over her chest. Though she'd stopped pacing, she hadn't sat down. Prior to spending time with Adelia, Fletcher wasn't used to being in a room with a woman where she was standing and he wasn't. "Do you always present your orders with flowers?"

Fletcher put down his glass and stood up. Though she was tall for a woman, he still had a few inches over her. Now that he was reminded of the fact that she'd gone to the party without him, and had been in the company of Jackson and Morrissey, he found his anger was trickling back.

"Whether it comes with flowers or in my own blood, if you are issued orders I expect you to abide by them."

Her eyes flashed in the lamp light. "Meri never gave me orders."

"Meri wasn't your superior."

Adelia took a step forward. Fletcher fought the urge to retreat. "And you think you are?"

"Where the Agency is concerned? Absolutely."

"But it's not just the Agency, is it? You think you're superior to everyone."

She'd taken another step forward and the front of her dress was very nearly brushing his jacket. Actually, he couldn't confirm that their clothing wasn't in fact touching, not without looking down and that was dangerous. Her brandy-brown eyes flashed. She was beautiful, of course, but here, in front of him without her usual detached, public facade, she was breathtaking.

"I don't think I'm superior to you." His voice was hoarse, like the words had been forced out. Her lips parted on a small gasp.

Fletcher wasn't entirely certain how it happened. One moment they were looking at each other, the next she was in his arms and his lips were on hers.

The kiss couldn't have lasted longer than a few seconds. Fletcher's wits finally returned and he dropped his arm. Adelia looked up at him, her eyes wide. She took a step back.

"I should retire," she said, turning away. She gave him a hurried good night over her shoulder and went to her rooms.

Fletcher remained in front of the fireplace, watching the door close behind her. He'd just made a huge mess of things when she was finally starting to show her trust. What was wrong with him?

CHAPTER THIRTEEN

Adelia wasn't surprised to see a note waiting for her the next morning.

After a fitful night's rest, she'd awoken wondering how on earth she was going to face Fletcher when next she saw him. She could have kicked herself for her behavior. She'd put in all that effort to show him he needed to treat her with proper respect, and what had it mattered when she'd gone and kissed him?

Or maybe he'd kissed her.

It didn't matter. She certainly hadn't minded.

With a deep breath, Adelia had opened the door to the drawing room only to let out a sigh of relief when Myles had handed her a note from Fletcher. At least, she'd told herself she was relieved.

She knew he was leaving town. A tiny part of her had hoped he would wait to see her before he left, but she pushed that thought down. Too foolish to consider.

I could never care for someone like you.

The words Fletcher had spoken in the vision came back to haunt her. Whatever temporary insanity they'd shared, Adelia couldn't allow herself to lose sight of the fact that someone like him could never truly have feelings for someone like her.

In the note, he had requested that she have an early night and return to the hotel after her performance.

Adelia should have bristled at the orders, but the idea of coming home after her performance that evening was too tempting. Maybe she'd have a bath. Even read a book.

She fetched her journal while Lilah ordered a breakfast tray and Adelia sat at the table in the drawing room, in the nook in front of the window. She'd decided to keep a record of her visions. She wasn't sure she believed that what she saw was true, but perhaps her mind was trying to tell her something. If she couldn't stop the visions completely, perhaps writing about them would give her some respite.

There was a knock on the door and Adelia looked up as Lilah went to get it. Instead of a breakfast tray, she returned with an envelope.

"It's from Renata," Adelia said, giving the note a quick review. "She is wondering if I am free to see her this afternoon to review lines."

"But you've hardly had a free moment since we arrived in Belfast."

Adelia was already heading to a desk to write a response. "Perhaps, but I'm not used to sitting around and because of Lord Fletcher's presence I've hardly spent any time with the cast."

"You see them every evening."

"I don't see them, Miranda does," Adelia said as she scribbled a reply and handed it over to Lilah. "Could you have this delivered please?"

Lilah pressed her lips together and took the note. She knew when a case was lost.

Adelia picked out a lavender day dress, one of the few dresses she owned that wasn't in a shade of pink or red, and headed out to the theater.

Since she had extra time, she decided to take a longer route. Without the aether fumes, the walk through the Belfast streets was quite pleasant and at one point Adelia was very nearly certain that the sun was peeking through the overcast sky. Like London there was a contrast between neighborhoods, the main difference being that the wealthy here were very well off. The grand houses were in excellent condition without so much as a shutter out of place.

Adelia was reminded again of the cost of the war with the Americas. Ireland had somehow managed to stay mostly neutral throughout the conflict—with only the east getting involved near the end to throw their weight behind a truce.

Britain had had a sort of alliance with them ever since, though Western Ireland was much more independent and even hosted groups like the Amer-Irish Guard who wanted the country to form an alliance with the Americas.

Adelia walked past a large mint green mansion that reminded her of a flavored ice, and turned onto the road that would take her to the theater. She went in through a side door that took her right to the backstage area.

During the run of a show there were always people at work during the day, fixing sets or mending costumes. Adelia saw Beulah sitting with another woman darning men's shirts.

"That's quite the pile," Adelia said, pointing at the basket.

"You wouldn't believe how hard the lads are on their costumes," Beulah said.

Given how much Mr. Davis loved stage fights, Adelia wouldn't have been surprised if the shirts ended up in the rag bin before the end of the run.

"Have you seen Renata today?"

Beulah nodded. "She was on the main stage last I saw."

"Thanks." Adelia adjusted her reticule where she had a copy of *The Tempest* just in case Renata wanted to review her role as understudy.

Adelia knew first-hand the value of being prepared. She'd gotten her big break as an understudy and had been given less than fifteen minutes notice to get herself on stage as Juliet.

She walked over to the wings of stage right and stopped when she saw Renata standing center stage. Adelia watched as the young woman took a step forward and began to speak.

"Oh wonder! How many goodly creatures are there here? How beauteous mankind is! Oh brave new world, that has such people in it."

Renata paused and looked to the shadows of stage left where Calen O'Donnell emerged.

"That was much better," Calen said, joining Renata on stage. "Though again, you must remember how naive Miranda is. Your words have a bit too much power."

Adelia had to admit that Calen's advice was good. The

one thing Renata lacked as an actress was subtlety. It was a conversation Adelia had had with her multiple times and she was glad Calen was reinforcing it.

"Before you try it again, I want you to really focus on thinking about things from Miranda's perspective."

"You think that's what Adelia has that I'm missing?"

Calen peered into the wing of stage right and grinned. "Why don't we ask her? Miss Dumont, won't you join us?"

As Adelia walked out on stage she noticed that Renata's cheeks turned bright pink. Adelia gave her friend a reassuring smile. There was no reason to feel guilty about practicing—it wasn't as though Adelia owned the part of Miranda.

"I think you're making excellent progress," Adelia said. "Mr. O'Donnell is giving you good advice."

"I am blessed to be surrounded by such talent," Calen said, making a sweeping gesture encompassing both women. Renata giggled and Adelia was glad to see her get over her embarrassment.

"Oh good, my two stars are here." Both Calen and Adelia turned to see Mr. Davis emerge from stage left. Renata took a step back, but didn't leave. "I have the best news. The British Ambassador to Ireland will be arriving in two days time and he's come specifically to see our show."

"He's making the trip just to see a play?" Calen asked.

"That's what we've been told." Mr. Davis clapped his hands. "He's sure to have an entourage. I imagine he'll be particularly impressed with how you've integrated into the cast, Calen."

"I can't wait to meet him," Calen said in such a convincing voice that it was clear he was as good an actor off stage as on.

"We can discuss it over lunch," Mr. Davis said. "You and Adelia can join me."

"I already have plans," Adelia said. "With Renata."

"Just the boys then," Mr. Davis clapped Calen on the back, leading him off stage.

"You could have gone," Renata said, her eyes on Calen's retreating form. "I would have understood."

"But I have plans with you," Adelia said. Not to mention, she found Mr. Davis tedious at the best of times. When he had something he was excited about he was even worse.

There was a noise from stage right and Adelia could see that several crew members were carrying out pieces of the shipwreck scene.

"Perhaps we should go to your dressing room?" Renata asked.

"Agreed."

Adelia led the way through the backstage and into the hallway that led to the dressing room. Beulah came out just as Adelia and Renata were about to enter.

"I just laid out your costumes for this evening," Beulah said. "And there was a flower delivery for you so I laid it on your dressing table."

"Really?" Adelia felt her lips pull into a smile. Fletcher had thought about her after all. She left Beulah and Renata chatting in the hall and went straight to her dressing table.

There were no pink roses this time. Instead these flowers were clusters of white buds and were unlike anything Adelia had ever seen. She picked them up to look for a note and a metallic scent filled her nostrils. Her head started to tingle.

"Are you all right?" Renata called from the doorway. "You look pale."

Adelia grabbed onto the excuse. "I think I'm getting a migraine. I should go back to the hotel."

"I'll go with you," Renata said, following her out of the dressing room. Company was the last thing she needed.

"No, I'll be fine, really. I just need some air."

Adelia didn't wait for Renata's response. She hurried backstage, nearly colliding with one of the crewmen, and burst out through the sidedoor. She dug through her reticule for the blockers and put one in her mouth, forcing herself to take deep breaths. Her vision stayed clear, but the worst headache was blooming behind her eyes. She needed to get back to Lilah.

From his seat in the dining room of the Briarwood Inn, Fletcher caught a glimpse of the ocean out of a bay window. If there was a bad view in the town, he'd yet to see it.

Which was why it was so odd that there weren't more tourists around. In London, with the Season drawing to a close, a town like this would have been overrun with gentry looking for an escape to the country. But as he ate his lunch in the relative silence of the drawing room, Fletcher noted there appeared to be no other visitors at the inn.

He asked the innkeeper about it as he paid his bill.

"We don't see as many guests as some of the other resort towns," the Innkeeper agreed with Fletcher's assessment, though the man refused to make eye contact. "But we make a decent living."

Fletcher nodded at the man as he left the inn, more convinced than ever that things weren't as they seemed. After all, what sort of innkeeper would be satisfied with no guests?

The story was the same in the few shops he visited. Fletcher would mention the lack of customers and the shopkeepers would reassure him that they got by just fine. There was one exception.

The bookshop was run by a middle aged woman with a mop of curly red hair. She smiled with relief when Fletcher walked into the store.

"A customer at last!" She said. "How can I help you?"

Fletcher grasped for a name and remembered his conversation with Adelia on the airship. "Do you have anything by D.A. Fitzgerald?"

"I've got his latest, hold on."

The woman nodded and disappeared into the back of the small shop. Fletcher took a moment to look around. While the store was quite small, every space was crowded with books. Fletcher had never seen so many titles in such a small space. He thought of Adelia and he wondered how she'd react to all the books.

When the shopkeeper returned, Fletcher was pleased to see it was a title he hadn't read and he chatted with the shopkeeper—who introduced herself as Wilma—while she wrapped up his purchase in brown paper. She seemed just as interested in the company as she was in having a paying customer.

"We only set up a few months back, my husband and I. We thought it was a golden opportunity—a resort town with no bookshop. What do people do when they come away for a break?"

"They read?" Fletcher offered and Wilma nodded, her curls springing around her head.

"But if no one comes to town, there's no one to buy books."

"Are you telling me no one visits at all?"

"A few stragglers. And there's the patients who come through every few months, but bless them, they're in no state to read."

Fletcher's ears perked up as she held his parcel out by the strings. "Patients?"

"I've heard they suffer from the fever." Wilma crossed herself as she spoke. "I heard a rumor that that's how the other shops manage—the crowd that takes care of the girls gives them money when they come through for supplies and such."

"What about the inn? I noticed it was empty."

"I'm friendly with the innkeeper's wife and she told me they get a fee from the lady's institute for keeping their rooms free just in case they have doctors and caregivers coming and going at short notice. They take in travellers of course, but never advertise. That's the agreement. Can you imagine? An inn being paid for empty rooms?"

Fletcher could imagine it, if the people paying wanted to keep strangers from spending time in the town.

"The travellers coming and going from the inn, are

they British?"

Wilma thought for a moment. "Mainly Westerners, you can tell by the way they draw out their a's and o's. So musical."

"Indeed." Fletcher said, his mind whirling. "Is the border that close?"

"It's a good day's drive, but when the races are happening that's nothing. People come from all over."

"How about the patients? Have you seen any of them out and about lately?"

"Oh no, we only see them when they are coming through town. Once they're set up in the institute—that's the large blue house on the next corner—they don't come out much."

Fletcher nodded at the woman. "Thank you for the books."

"Come back anytime!"

Fletcher had the carriage stop at the side of the road so that he could get out and look over the edge of a cliff. The town was definitely keeping secrets. He'd passed by the blue house Wilma had referred to, but there was no one outside and all the curtains were drawn at all the windows. He didn't want to draw attention to himself, so he'd continued on his way, just a gentleman on a leisurely walk.

From where he was standing on the cliff, Fletcher could see a small port below—presumably where the girls arrived. There was one decent sized ship and several small fishing boats. He was about to go back to his carriage, it was getting late and he needed to formulate a plan before returning, when something truly strange caught his eye.

The larger boat was flying a flag that Fletcher was fairly certain was used by retired British navy men.

Fletcher took out his notebook and took a quick sketch. He knew just who to send the drawing to.

CHAPTER FOURTEEN

Adelia had never missed a show, and she wasn't about to start now, but getting through her performance that evening had been one of her most difficult experiences as an actress.

Lilah had tried to talk her out of going, reminding her that this was why she had an understudy. But though it might seem vain, Adelia knew that part of the reason the performances were selling out was because she was the lead female in the show.

As a compromise, Lilah had accompanied her to the theater and had prepared a tea that helped with the worst of the headache, at least for a short period of time. Adelia had told her maid about the strange flowers that seemed to have triggered the migraine and Lilah had gone ahead to the dressing room but the flowers had already been removed.

As soon as she took her final bow, Adelia went to her dressing room to change. Mr. Davis had been unimpressed with her message that she would not be making an appearance in the green room and had come down to her dressing room himself to change her mind. However, it was Lilah who'd intervened.

"I have instructions from Lord Fletcher himself that Miss Dumont is to go straight back to the hotel," Lilah had informed him. At her words Mr. Davis had backed off immediately.

Myles fetched a carriage to take her back to the hotel and Adelia hadn't had the energy to fight them about the short walk. She made it up the stairs and into the drawing room where she'd dropped onto the sofa nearest the fireplace while Lilah had gone to get her more tea.

She must have fallen asleep, because the next thing Adelia became aware of was the sensation that someone was standing over her. She opened her eyes to find Fletcher next to the sofa.

"I must have drifted off," Adelia said, pushing herself into a sitting position.

"Lilah told me you are unwell," Fletcher said. "You look pale."

"I'm fine," Adelia said, reaching for the tea Lilah had left for her on the side table. It must have been sitting out for a few minutes, but it was still warm enough to drink.

Fletcher finally moved to sit on the sofa across from her, his eyes on her as she sipped her tea.

"You came home with a migraine this afternoon?"

Adelia pursed her lips. "Apparently Lilah's feeling chatty."

"She was worried about you. She said you aren't usually prone to illness."

"I'm not." She put down her tea cup. The worst of the headache had subsided but she felt like she could sleep for hours.

"Did something happen?"

For a moment Adelia wondered if she should share her suspicions with him. Would he think she was mentally unwell? But then she dismissed the thought. He already knew she suffered from the fever and so far he hadn't held it against her.

"There was a flower delivery to my dressing room. When I picked it up, my head started to tingle and I very nearly had a vision right there and then."

"But you didn't?"

Adelia shook her head. "I suppressed it, but that's when the headache came on."

Fletcher leaned forward, resting his elbows on his knees. It was a remarkably casual posture. His brown hair fell across his forehead and Adelia was struck by an urge to push the locks back. Now that her headache was dissipating, she recalled her earlier reluctance with seeing Fletcher again. The last time they'd been together, they'd shared a kiss—in this very room.

She reached for her teacup to hide the blush she could feel creeping up her face.

"One of our agents reported an airborne mist that brought on the visions," Fletcher said. "Perhaps this flower is an ingredient in the mist. You didn't recognize the plant?"

Adelia shook her head. She was grateful that Fletcher didn't seem to suffer from the same discomfort over their shared moment of intimacy. But a small part of her wondered why he was so unaffected. She pushed that thought down. It wasn't important.

"I'm not good with plants but if I saw it again, I think

I would recognize it."

"That's a start," Fletcher said, straightening back up in his chair. "I suppose you have no idea who the flowers were from?"

"I thought they might be from you, but there was no note."

"I always send roses."

Adelia found she was quite keen to know how often he sent roses to women, but again, she reminded herself to stay focused.

"When we returned to the theater this evening, the flowers were gone. I'm sorry I wasn't in a position to take a sample."

He frowned, his lips forming a thin, tense line. "Well I suppose we have confirmation now that someone knows about your condition. We have to assume that's why you were sent the flowers."

Adelia felt a sudden chill despite being so close to the fireplace.

"But I was at the theater, in the middle of the day."

"Which means Jackson has a spy. If he's working with James Morrissey it would be easy enough for them to ask someone working at the theater his father owns to keep an eye on you."

"That's a horrible thought."

"From now on you go nowhere alone, is that clear?"

"I don't think we need to go that far—"

But Fletcher wasn't having any part of her objections. "That's an order, Adelia."

She wanted to argue, but her eyes felt heavy. "Could we continue our conversation in the morning? I'm still a little tired."

"We can, but it won't change anything." Fletcher got to his feet, his scowl slipped into a look of concern. He walked over to her sofa and held out a hand. "Let me help you to your room."

Fletcher figured he'd been in and out of every flower shop in Belfast. He'd risen early to send Meri a telegram about the flag he'd seen in Briarwood and had returned to the hotel to see if Adelia was available to identify flowers. If they could find the shop, they might be able to ask for a description of the sender.

It was a long shot.

"Still nothing?" he asked Adelia as she looked over the display behind the counter. She shook her head.

"No. I don't see it."

They left the florist and headed down the street toward a tea shop. Since it was midday, the shop was fairly busy, but a waiter led them to a table next to a window.

"I'm sorry I wasn't much help," Adelia said after they placed their order. "I've never been much for flowers."

As usual, she was dressed in shades of pink. She looked out the window, watching the people go past while Fletcher's focus was on her.

He'd thought he was over the kiss they'd shared. It was obviously a temporary slip, something that happened as a result of spending too much time together. But then he'd come home the night before and Adelia had been asleep on the drawing room sofa, strands of hair covering her face; it had taken all of his willpower not to move those locks.

"I can hardly blame you," Fletcher said, forcing himself back to the present moment. "I'm much more at home in a bookstore."

The corner of Adelia's mouth quirked into the beginning of a smile. "I never would have taken you for a great reader."

"Hardly," Fletcher snorted at the thought. "I lost my way in novels, not academic works. It was an interest I shared with my father."

It was perhaps the greatest interest he shared with his father, but Fletcher didn't add that.

"Well, I can do you one better," Adelia said. "I was practically raised in a bookshop."

"And here I'd believed the rumor that you'd been born on a stage."

"Not quite," Adelia said, and some of the sparkle went out of her eyes. He wanted to bring it back.

"Tell me about the bookshop."

Adelia appeared to think for a moment, then a small smile formed in the corners of her lips. "It was my uncle's shop. He inherited it from my grandfather and my father worked there with him. It was located in the east end."

"Really?" Fletcher straightened. "There were several shops we visited in the east end. What was it called?"

"Montgomery Books."

"No, really? I spent so much time there. It was my favorite—" Fletcher stopped as he remembered the shop's fate.

"Until the fire," Adelia finished. "My uncle and father both perished."

Fletcher remembered the heartache he'd had over the

tragic loss of the store. For Adelia, she'd lost family as well.

The waiter returned with a tea tray and Adelia seemed keen to grab onto a new topic.

"Did you find anything useful in your travels yesterday?" She asked.

"Actually, I think there's definitely something going on in Briarwood."

Adelia stopped with a cup halfway to her face. "Why didn't you say something right away? When are you going back?"

"I think I'll wait until your run is complete and perhaps stay back a few days to check things out."

Adelia narrowed her eyes. "You want to send me back home so you can do the real work?"

"No, that's not it at all. But after what happened yesterday, I won't risk leaving you alone again."

"Why don't I come with you? It's far less suspicious than you staying behind in Belfast on your own. Besides, I have the day off Sunday. It's perfectly natural that we take a drive around the country."

"Fair enough," Fletcher agreed. By then Meri should have gotten back to him. "I will warn you that it's quite a lot of time in a carriage, especially if we are going to attempt to make the trip in one day."

"Don't worry, I'm up for it." She picked up the pot of jam. "I forgot to tell you, the British Ambassador to Ireland is coming to see a show."

"Indeed? You must tell me all about Davis' reaction. I assume he was beside himself."

"But of course." Adelia grinned and regaled him with the details.

CHAPTER FIFTEEN

Adelia woke early Sunday morning and decided on a yellow day dress and jacket. Normally, with her blond hair, she would have avoided the color, but Madame de Meliodor had permitted this particular shade because the gold undertones complimented her coloring.

"You look like a ray of sunshine," Lilah said, handing over her reticule. "Are you quite certain you don't want me to accompany you today?"

"I am," Adelia said, looking herself over in the mirror and adjusting the wide brimmed straw hat on her head. "What's more, I would like you to take today to do something for yourself."

Lilah's eyes lit up. "Really?"

Adelia took in her maid's excited expression and wondered if perhaps she'd make plans with Myles. While she was glad Lilah had made a friend, she hoped the two weren't overly attached. After all, once they returned to London they'd be going in separate directions.

Fletcher was waiting for Adelia when she entered the drawing room and he looked her over with a nod of approval.

"I think that's the perfect ensemble for a day trip."

Adelia felt her cheeks heat at his approving gaze—which she reminded herself was foolish.

"Shall we?" Fletcher held an arm out to her and they left the suite, heading down the stairs to the carriage he'd arranged for the day.

"I wish it was warm enough to travel in one of those roofless carriages," Adelia said as she settled into the seat across for Fletcher. "But at least we can open the windows."

Adelia gazed out the window, watching the city go by. She'd taken her hat off and, along with a novel, it occupied the seat next to her while Fletcher sat across from her in brown trousers and a matching jacket and moss green cravat that gave his brownish eyes a hazel hue.

"It is a nice change from London," Fletcher said.

"It is, but I'll be happy to return home," Adelia said. "Much as I appreciate the adventure."

"With any luck we won't have any missions for a while. Assuming we're successful here."

"Really?" Adelia leaned forward. "You truly believe there aren't any other threats?"

"There are always threats, but most of the Agency's work has been focused on neutralizing whoever's behind the abductions. I think there'll be, at least, a bit of a lull."

Though his words indicated he was relieved to have a break, Adelia got the impression that something was weighing on his mind. She noticed he had a new D.A. Fitzgerald novel so she moved the conversation to their common love of books.

They stopped once to stretch their legs and fell into a

quiet hour while they both read. Once they arrived at Briarwood, Fletcher suggested they have lunch at the inn.

"There's no one here," Adelia said in a low voice as
they were seated at a table near a window. The sun was
peeking out from behind the clouds and rays streamed in
across their table.

"It was the same the last time I was here," Fletcher
said. "The food was impeccable, but there were no other
diners."

The innkeeper came to take their order. He looked
Fletcher over, obviously remembering him from his last
visit, but didn't engage him in any unnecessary conversation. Soon they were alone in the dining room and Adelia
imagined what it would be like if they were what they
appeared to be on the outside—just a couple, spending an
afternoon together, courting.

Of course, that was an outrageous thought. For one
thing, Fletcher could never court a woman like her. For
another, they had a job to do.

"What's the plan?" Adelia asked. "I assume you have
one?"

"I'd like to visit the docks," Fletcher said. "There's a
retired British naval officer who I think might be living
there."

"Is he trustworthy?" Adelia asked.

"Meri indicated that he was."

"You've been in contact with Meri?"

"Just once," Fletcher said. Adelia noted that his lips
thinned slightly when she asked about their common
friend. "Shall we go?"

Instead of going straight to the port, Fletcher took a detour to the bookshop. The shopkeeper looked up from her counter and grinned.

"You again!"

Fletcher knew he'd made the right decision by returning there first.

"I'm honored you remembered my visit."

"As I said, we don't get many customers around here." The shopkeeper turned her attention to Adelia, who was running a finger over the spine of a book, a look of delight on her face.

"Who might this be?" Wilma nodded at Adelia. "A sweetheart perhaps?"

"Something like that." Adelia turned to her, the smile slipping just a little. "You have a lovely shop here. I've never seen so many books in such a small space."

"Our Bristol shop was much bigger," the shopkeeper explained, pushing a stray lock of red hair back off her face. "When we came here we tried to fit as much of our stock as possible in the new space."

"And what brought you here?" Adelia asked, picking a novel off the shelf. She soon had the shopkeeper engaged in a conversation about her life before coming to the resort town.

Pleased with how well Adelia was doing, Fletcher focused on Wilma's answers; paying attention to her tone of voice. His instincts didn't waiver from his last encounter in the shop. Whatever else was going on in the town, he felt he could trust the shopkeeper.

"And what of the other businesses?" Adelia continued. "Are they new as well?"

"No, not at all," the shopkeeper shook her head, the gesture causing stray curls to bob around her face. "Everyone else set up right from the start, when the resort first opened."

"Indeed?" Fletcher asked.

"That's what made us want to come here. Don't often get a resort town with such little turnover. We didn't realize hardly anyone came through, not even during the races."

"What are the races?" Adelia asked.

Wilma explained about the nearby racing arena that hosted seasonal events.

"There's one here next week," Wilma said. "Not that it will do us much good. All the other resort towns host events to go with the races so all the tourists flock there instead."

"That's unfortunate," Adelia said. "Have you ever thought of doing anything here?"

"You come with an idea that'll draw a crowd and this bookshop will sponsor it. That's a promise."

"I think I'll get these books," Adelia said, setting two volumes on the counter and reaching for her coin purse.

"Allow me," Fletcher stepped forward. Adelia looked as though she was about to object, but Fletcher shook his head ever so slightly. He thought she was going to argue but instead, she waited until they were outside before she turned on him.

"I can pay for my own books."

"I'm well aware of that," Fletcher said. "But since you're my sweetheart, it would be most unusual to allow you to do that. We don't need to raise any more alarms than necessary."

"Of course," Adelia said, deflating slightly as her anger seeped away. "I'll pay you back."

"You won't," Fletcher said. "Consider it an Agency expense."

Adelia looked as though she were about to argue again, but then something caught her eye as they made their way back toward the inn and she pointed at the garden on the side of the large blue house on the corner.

"Those are the flowers," she said. "I'm certain of it."

Fletcher moved toward the fence and reached down, picking a daisy. He didn't want to touch the flower he'd suspected had given Adelia such a terrible headache, but at the same time he didn't want to risk drawing attention their way if anyone happened to be watching them.

"I believe this is where the girls are being kept." He held the daisy out to Adelia. She took it with a smile, letting anyone watching them think they were a couple out for a walk.

Adelia glanced up at the windows which were once again blocked off by curtains. "What should we do?"

"I'll collect a sample of the other flower before we head out, but I won't bring it in the carriage with us."

He held out his arm to her, and Adelia took it.

"Could we stop just there, by the fence post. We should be able to see the water from there." They paused at the post and Adelia inhaled sharply. "This is the view from my vision—the first one with Mr. Jackson."

Fletcher nodded ever so slightly. "We should keep going. In case someone is watching."

The walk to the dock was picturesque and would have been downright pleasant if they'd arrived under other circumstances. The sun was fully out and the water fairly sparkled as the rays reflected off the waves.

The dock area wasn't large, as befitted a small town and unlike the busy ports of the cities, they weren't overwhelmed by the stench of old fish and rotting vegetables.

"Who are we looking for?" Adelia asked.

As she spoke, a head popped up from an opening in the deck and a gray-haired gentleman dressed in the navy blue of a sea captain emerged.

"Who goes there?" he called in a gruff voice. Fletcher noted that he had a British accent with no hint of an Irish lilt.

"Hello, we're looking for Captain Cartright," Fletcher called.

"Never asked who you were looking for," the man called back. "I asked for names."

"I'm Lord Fletcher and this is my companion, Miss Adelia Dumont."

The man's bushy gray eyebrows scrunched together. "Not the actress?"

Adelia took a step forward. "You've heard of me?"

The man fully emerged from below deck and hurried over to the railing where he squinted down at them. "It is you! I saw you as Ophelia, must be two years back. The Hamlet was awful, but you were an absolute delight."

Adelia grinned. "That was my first starring role."

"You wait there and I'll be right down."

Fletcher leaned close to Adelia. "It appears you have a fan."

The man settled in front of them. He wasn't tall, but he more than made up for it in bearing.

"I'm Captain Cartright. Now tell me what brings you to my docks?"

"We have a common friend—Captain Merritt Lancaster."

"Captain now, is it? Bit young isn't he?"

Fletcher caught Adelia suppressing a laugh.

"He assures me you are completely to be trusted," Fletcher continued. "I hope that's the case."

The captain looked Fletcher over again with narrowed eyes.

"What did you say your business was here?"

"We didn't," Adelia said, taking a step forward. "But perhaps there's someplace we could talk?"

Fletcher watched the captain's face, certain he was about to tell them to leave but he gave a quick nod instead.

"You'd best come in then."

They followed the captain back to the small vessel. There was a gangway leading from the dock to the deck and the captain held out a hand to assist Adelia, leaving Fletcher to follow behind, listening in on their conversation as they made their way into the vessel's interior.

"I never was much of one for sitting still," Captain Cartright explained as they settled into what must serve as his living quarters on board. He offered Adelia one of two chairs set at a round wooden table, leaving Fletcher standing in the doorway. "But I went to see that play twice."

"I'm glad you enjoyed it," Adelia said as the captain

went to the corner and pulled the lid off a potbelly stove. He poked at the flames and set a kettle to boil before taking the seat across from Adelia. She told him about the show in Belfast and invited him to come see it.

"I'll give it some thought," the captain said, looking to Fletcher. "Now, are you going to tell me what brings you here?"

Fletcher took a step forward, reaching into his inside pocket and produced three small portraits. "Have you seen any of these ladies around town?"

The captain held up each picture at arms length. He put two down on the table next to him, but continued looking at the one he held in his hand. "I may have, but not for a while."

"How about this one?" Adelia took a miniature from her reticule and slid it across the table. Fletcher wondered where she'd gotten it from, but he'd have to ask her about it later.

"Now this one I saw last week," the captain said, tapping his finger on the glass inside the frame.

Fletcher tried not to show his excitement. Could they have cracked the case this quickly?

"Why are you looking for her?"

"We'd like to return her to her parents," Fletcher said.

"Return her? If her parents didn't send her here then who did?"

Fletcher scratched his ear, trying to decide how much to reveal, but Adelia leaned forward in her chair.

"Do you know anything about the big blue house, the one just up from the inn?"

The captain nodded. "I know the one. Some kind of

institute. That's what the villagers say."

"What do you say?" Fletcher asked.

"I say it's the only thing in this village that makes any sense. The inn is always empty, the stock barely moves in the general store, but that school seems to be well attended. Girls always coming and going."

"You've seen them leave?" Adelia asked.

"I've taken them back to England myself," the captain said. "Though, only on the rare occasion. Usually they hire their own conveyance."

"You've taken them back to England?" Fletcher asked. "Are you certain?"

The captain scowled. "I think I would remember if I'd brought them somewhere else."

"Do the girls ever leave the institute?" Adelia asked. The captain's expression softened again as he looked back to her.

"They walk through town once a day, usually first thing in the morning. And of course they attend church on Sundays. But otherwise, they keep very much to themselves."

"Would you believe me if I told you at least one of these girls was here without the knowledge of her family?"

The captain frowned. "I don't know much, but those girls appear to be well looked after."

"But have you ever seen any family around?"

"Well, no," the captain conceded. "But I assumed that's because they are so far away."

A cloud of steam came out the spout of the kettle and Captain Cartright got up to prepare a pot of tea.

"Do you know when the girls are heading back to England?"

"Of course, it'll be the evening of the big race."

"You know that for certain?" Fletcher asked. The captain looked up from the stove.

"They always move the girls during the races. I figured because it's easier to get big ships in and out during that time—lots of people want to be around these parts for the races."

"And the next race is a week away?" Fletcher asked.

"That's right," the captain said, bringing the teapot and mismatched cups back to the table. He turned his attention back to Adelia. "It's unfortunate that you can't bring a performance here."

"Perhaps we can," Fletcher said, though neither Adelia nor the captain were paying him any attention.

CHAPTER SIXTEEN

The sun was low in the sky when they got in the carriage to head back to Belfast, but there was still enough light for reading. Adelia found she didn't mind the long ride back in a comfortable carriage with fresh air and new books. She'd just opened the cover on a brand new mystery, when Fletcher leaned forward, his elbows resting on his knees.

"What would you think of doing a performance in Briarwood?"

Adelia closed her book. "Are you being serious?"

"We need a reason to go back to the village," Fletcher said. "And this could be the distraction needed to help rescue the women from the institute there."

"It's an interesting idea." Adelia tapped the cover of her book. "What did you think of Captain Cartright's claim that the women went back to England?"

"Honestly?" Fletcher leaned back on his bench. "I don't get the impression he's lying, but it doesn't make sense. If a group like the Amer-Irish Guard has figured that these women have special abilities, why take them away from England just to send them back?"

Adelia shivered, she couldn't help it. "If the Guard are involved, they must have a reason for sending the women back rather than bringing them over the border."

Fletcher clapped his hands together. "We need to find out what's happening in the big blue house. If the women can tell us what has been happening to them, maybe we can figure out why they're being sent back."

"We've come all this way to find out there are women back in England," Adelia said with a shake of her head.

"Ironic, isn't it? But we still have a job here. I'll talk to Davis about bringing a few company members out to Briarwood. When he hears about the crowd who come for the races, I imagine he'll be beside himself with enthusiasm. And while the crowds are watching you, we'll use the distraction of all the extra foot traffic to intercept the women at the dock."

"I don't think we could do a full production," Adelia said, giving it some thought. "There doesn't appear to be a space for that. But perhaps some recitations? All that would require is a large room."

Fletcher nodded, his eyes alight. "That's a perfect idea. I'm sure there's a local bookstore that would love to sponsor the event."

"Giving us even more reason to be in the community leading up to the event."

They continued making plans, even going so far as to pick out potential selections for Adelia to recite, when they arrived back in Belfast.

"We can continue our talk over supper?" Fletcher asked as he helped her down from the carriage."

"Yes, that would be lovely," Adelia agreed, taking his arm as they walked up the stairs to the main doors.

Despite the fact that they were on an important mission, Adelia found that she was filled with a warm contentedness that she hadn't felt in a long time, and certainly never in the presence of a man like Lord Fletcher.

But then, she was starting to believe he wasn't at all as she'd originally been led to believe.

They had just entered the lobby when Fletcher halted abruptly at her side and she had to stop herself or risk tripping.

"Apologies," Fletcher said, giving her a brief glance before turning his attention back to an elderly man with a pasty complexion that could only be rivaled by milled flour.

"My Lord," the man said, approaching him with a bowed head.

"Wilson," Fletcher said, his voice colder than Adelia had ever heard it. "What are you doing here?"

"Forgive me for interrupting your evening," the man said, his watering eyes narrowing on Adelia. She stiffened her spine, all the warmth she'd been feeling draining out of her body. "But I'm here at your mother's bequest. She would like to dine with you this evening at the Emerald Hotel."

Adelia felt Fletcher's arm flinch beneath her gloved hand. Whatever was happening here, it had caught him unaware.

"My mother is in Belfast?"

"Lady Fletchingham arrived this afternoon by private airship at the special invitation of the Ambassador."

For a moment Adelia thought Fletcher was going to lose his temper at the man. His nostrils flared but as he continued speaking, his voice was calm.

"You can tell my mother that I will expect a private audience with her in half an hour."

"I will deliver your message without delay."

Adelia half expected to hear a creaking sound as the man bowed. Once they were alone, Fletcher led her to the stairs and up to their suite.

"I think you should go ahead and dine without me," Fletcher said, his voice was detached as he spoke, as though he was no longer still in her presence. "It appears I have some personal business to take care of and I don't know how long it will take."

"I'll make notes while you are gone," Adelia said, making an effort to keep her voice light. "That way we can speak about our plans either later this evening or over breakfast in the morning."

"Thank you," Fletcher said. "That's an excellent idea."

As she moved her hand, releasing his arm, Fletcher took her gloved fingers, raising them to his lips before heading out the door. Adelia held up her fingers and found that the contented feeling hadn't been completely lost after all.

Fletcher asked for directions to The Emerald Hotel, but did not take the doorman up on his offer to find him a carriage. He needed to calm down before he spoke to his mother or he risked saying something that truly couldn't be taken back.

The evening air was misty, but since it wasn't filled with aether fumes, it didn't bother him. In fact, he would have asked Adelia to take a walk with him after supper if his mother hadn't come barrelling into his life.

The Emerald Hotel was taller and less sprawling than Hotel Donegall. Inside it lived up to its name with a lobby done up in deep green carpets and dark wood paneling. Fletcher figured the old fashioned style was probably more suited to his mother's taste. He gave his name at the front desk and was shown to a creaking monstrosity of an automatic lift.

"Her ladyship is on the top floor," the woman at the front desk told him. "Just punch the number seven and the automaton will do all the work."

It wasn't his first time on an automatic lift—London had them as well, but as the gilded gate closed in front of him, Fletcher thought to himself that he had never really considered how much the experience resembled walking into a crypt. Or perhaps the dreary thought was a result of what awaited him at the end of the ride.

At least this crypt was well lit.

The automaton in the lift was tall and narrow. Whereas most of the British models were short and squat, this one came almost to eye level. It was painted in green livery to match the hotel decor and had an egg shaped face with an open mouth and black eyes that stared straight ahead.

Fletcher found himself missing the friendly round automatons from home. At least they were short enough that he didn't have to look in their dead eyes.

Instead of brass buttons, the livery on the automaton's chest were elevator buttons. Fletcher hit the number seven and the lift made a groaning sound, as though it were an arthritic old man being forced to stand up.

"Going up," a mechanical voice boomed and Fletcher flung his hand over his chest before realizing there was a speaker in the automaton's open mouth.

The lift finally stopped and Fletcher opened the gate to a floor with one set of double doors. Of course Lady Fletchingham wouldn't share a floor with other guests.

Fletcher stepped up to the doors and knocked once. He wasn't surprised when Wilson opened the door revealing an elegant foyer in deep wood tones.

"Correct me if I am wrong," Fletcher said. "But I was under the impression you worked for me?"

WIlson bowed his head but refused to look contrite at Fletcher's chastisement. "As your lordship was away, I deferred to the direction of her ladyship."

"And where is my mother now?"

"She is in the drawing room, awaiting your arrival."

Fletcher followed Wilson down the carpeted hallway, to a set of French doors. Too late, Fletcher realized, there were multiple voices drifting out of the room.

Of course his mother wouldn't agree to meet him on her own.

With a sense of dread, Fletcher stepped into the drawing room. Like everything else in the hotel, it was decorated in colors that were much too dark, in this case forest greens and mahogany woods. Fletcher was immediately greeted by the Countess Sinclair and Lady Fianna.

Playing court in the middle of the room, seated in a green damask wingback chair, was his mother.

"Lord Fletchingham!" She called as though this was a happy meeting between family members. "I'm so glad you were able to pull yourself away from business to join us for supper."

Fletcher had intended to do no such thing. He'd planned on confronting his mother and then returning back to his own suite for a late meal. If Adelia was still up when he returned, then all the better.

Unfortunately, he felt well and truly trapped. The only good thing about the situation was that he'd managed to walk in right as the meal was starting, which meant he didn't need to spend a lot of time in the drawing room making small talk.

He was not surprised when his mother seated Lady Fianna to his right. As always, she was elegantly turned out in a pale evening gown in a shade of pink. Fletcher couldn't help thinking of Adelia and how the delicate color would have brought out the gold in her curls.

Since Fianna had no way of knowing his thoughts were on another young lady, she engaged Fletcher in conversation.

"Are you enjoying Belfast?"

"I'm enjoying the Irish air," Fletcher said. "As I imagine any Londoner would. Going out in a city without the worry of a mask is a refreshing experience."

"I wouldn't know," Lady Fianna shook her head. Fletcher noted that not one blond strand dared to come loose from her updo. "Mama has been very particular about not allowing me to go around the city without an escort."

Fletcher caught the frown that was about to form on his face just in time. Now that he knew Adelia's age to be near twenty-one, her independence was all the more remarkable.

"Well, I'm sure Fletcher will want to take you out to show you the sights," his mother spoke up from the other end of the table.

"Nothing would delight me more," Fletcher said. "If

only I had the time."

"We missed you very much in London this past week, Fletcher," the Countess said, taking her cue from his mother. "What sort of business brought you to Ireland?"

Fletcher was fairly certain his sudden decision to leave town to chase an actress had been discussed at length in every London ballroom, and while very young ladies were generally kept away from such gossip by overprotective mothers, Countess Sinclair had no doubt not only heard the rumors, but had likely helped spread them.

Which meant she was only asking him about his trip to give him an opportunity to present an appropriate reason for his presence in Belfast to her impressionable daughter.

"I'm pursuing some avenues of business," Fletcher said. "There's a nearby resort town I'm checking out. All very dull."

"Well, I hope you can spare some time for us tomorrow evening," his mother said. Fletcher was about to tell her he had plans when her next statement shook him. "We've been invited by the ambassador to share a box at the theater. I believe they're showing *The Tempest*."

"We've heard wonderful things about it," Fianna said. "But I suppose you've already seen it?"

"I can make time to go again," Fletcher said, his brain already trying to work out what possible motive his mother could have to risk exposing the woman she wanted him to marry to the woman she thought was his mistress.

"Then I look forward to a pleasant evening," Lady Fletchingham said, picking up her glass of claret with a nod in his direction.

CHAPTER SEVENTEEN

Adelia awoke the next morning still feeling the remnants of her good mood from the evening before.

Fletcher may have had to run out on their plans, and he may not have returned before she'd gone to bed for the evening, but they'd had a wonderful day together. It was almost like they were really becoming friends.

Adelia walked into the drawing room the next morning and was surprised to find Fletcher already there with a breakfast tray in front of him.

"Lilah told me you were already awake so I took the liberty of ordering breakfast."

Adelia sat across from him. She'd gone back to pinks this morning and it didn't escape her notice that Fletcher seemed to be particularly focussed on her dress.

"Is something wrong?" Adelia looked down at her skirt.

"No, just admiring the color on you."

She cleared her throat, reaching for the jam dish. She could feel the warmth flooding her cheeks.

"What's our plan for today?"

"I thought we could talk with Davis this morning,"

Fletcher said. "I already sent a note to his rooms to request a meeting."

"Excellent," Adelia said. "Is that coffee?"

"Yes, I can order tea if you'd prefer."

"Coffee is perfect." She poured herself a cup.

Fletcher waited while she added milk before continuing. "We can present him with the idea of doing a short set of readings. I am almost certain the bookshop will be on board as a sponsor."

"We'll have a week to prepare?"

"Yes, we'll want to be ready the evening of the races. Hopefully we can attract enough patrons to Briarwood that our rescue efforts will go unnoticed until it's too late."

"How will we get the ladies away? Are you thinking of asking Captain Cartright to help us?"

"Smitten with the old man, aren't you?" Fletcher teased. "No, his rig is too small and likely too slow. We'll need a quick escape. I've messaged Meri for assistance."

"He'll know what to do," Adelia agreed. "Do you think a few recitations will be enough to draw a crowd?"

"I have faith in you as our key attraction, though if a few more in the company want to join us, that would be helpful."

"It could be an opportunity for some of the less experienced company members," Adelia said. "Since they usually only get a line or two. My understudy in particular would love the opportunity."

"You have an understudy?" Fletcher raised an eyebrow.

"All lead actors have an understudy."

"Yes, but I can't imagine yours gets to work all that much."

Adelia cleared her throat and sipped her coffee. "I do my best to never let the patrons down."

"Because you know you are the reason they are coming to the theater."

"That's not what I said."

Fletcher grinned. It gave him a boyish appearance.

"You did say you didn't want to let the patrons down."

"Yes well, I'm sure they come for the other actors as well. It's an ensemble performance."

"Indeed," Fletcher said, the smile slipping from his face. "There's something we should discuss."

Adelia put down her coffee cup an ominous feeling washing over her at the serious look on Fletcher's face.

"As you are aware, my mother is in town."

"I hope you had a pleasant visit?"

"I did not, but that isn't relevant. The reason I am bringing her up this morning is that she has obtained a box for tonight's show."

"She knows the rumors about us?"

"I don't think it was possible for her not to," Fletcher said. "I made sure our cover was known all over London."

Adelia nodded, more to reassure herself than Fletcher. "That hardly affects me though. She's not likely to call me out while I'm on stage."

Fletcher's lips formed a thin line, but he didn't answer. Instead he tapped the side of his coffee cup. Once. Twice. Three times.

"What are you not telling me?" There had to be something. After all, this wasn't the first time she'd been in such a situation. Meri's mother had seen her in *The Taming of the Shrew* the year before and she must have suspected the same thing of her as Lady Fletchingham apparently did.

"My mother didn't come to Belfast alone."

"I wouldn't have thought she would. Is she traveling with her friends? I know ladies in her set can be quite stuck on proprieties."

"Her friends are among those she's travelling with. In particular is the Countess Sinclair who also brought her daughter."

Adelia froze. Not just in action, but her body grew cold all over. "And her daughter is someone special to you?"

"No, not at this time."

"But some future time?"

"That is my mother's hope."

"I see," Adelia said. And she did.

I could never care for someone like you.

"But my mother's wishes are not relevant. We're here for a case and that remains my priority."

"Then why tell me about any of this?"

"I thought it best you be prepared," Fletcher said. "In case you heard any rumors.

Adelia picked her napkin up off her lap and dropped it on the table. "Well, if there's nothing more to discuss, should we call on Mr. Davis?"

"Yes, we probably should."

Fletcher rose from the table to have a word with Myles. As he left, Adelia was immensely proud of herself for keeping her cool expression while inside, she was almost certain her heart had cracked open.

The last time Fletcher had been at the theater he had promised himself he wouldn't return until he could come back to watch Adelia perform by himself. Yet, here he was in a booth once more with perhaps even more tedious companions than on his last visit.

He'd avoided going to his mother's rooms beforehand, instead, sending her a note to tell her he was otherwise occupied and would meet her at the theater. If her expression upon greeting him were anything to go by, his note had not been well received.

"I've never seen a production of *The Tempest*," Lady Fianna said, fanning her face. "How do they make it look like there's a storm?"

"They use some very clever set design," Fletcher said. He'd taken the seat to Fianna's right because it had been the only one left when he'd arrived.

"I've seen Miss Dumont of course," Fianna said. "But I didn't find her nearly as impressive as I'd been led to believe."

"Did you not?" Fletcher asked, hoping the irritation that he felt hadn't come through in his voice.

"I thought she'd be so much more … dramatic," Fianna continued talking. "She was so subdued."

Fletcher was about to explain that it was her understated manner that made her so popular when he felt the poke of his mother's cane in his calf. He looked to his left but of course she was chatting with the countess and the ambassador—a portly man with a thick neck—as though nothing were amiss.

Fortunately, the lights went down before Fletcher was subjected to any further small talk.

Once the play started, Fletcher was swept along by the performance. Even though he'd seen the show before, Adelia's performance drew him in, making everything and everyone around him completely irrelevant in that moment.

When Adelia appeared on stage for the first time as Miranda, looking out at the wild waters, he could have sworn she was looking right at him.

Which was a ridiculous thought.

When the curtain came down at intermission, Fletcher found he needed a moment to reorient himself.

"Are you quite well?" Fianna asked, and Fletcher looked to the woman next to him. Once again he couldn't help the comparisons that leapt to mind. He was unsurprised to find Fianna dressed in a shade of pink—this time a deep rose—that he'd seen Adelia wear only days before. Yet the woman in front of him was like a delicate watercolor, showing no boldness or resolve.

It wasn't that Adelia was more attractive than Fianna, it was that she was more certain of herself. Adelia had an awareness of who she was while Lady Fianna was still a model created by the society in which they'd both grown up.

Was the same true for him? That was a jarring thought.

"In truth, you look a little pale," Fianna said, now looking about her, likely to catch his mother's attention, which was the last thing he wanted.

"Actually, I think I just need some air."

As Fletcher rose to his feet, Fianna did as well.

"Some fresh air would be lovely," she said, leaving Fletcher no choice but to hold out his arm and accompany her out of the box, catching his mother's nod of approval as they left.

Fletcher was surprised by Fianna's forwardness, but then as his mother's invited guest on a voyage away from home, she likely had it in her head that she was a real contender for the role of future wife.

Of course, if his mother had anything to say on the matter she would be.

"Are you enjoying the play?" Fletcher asked as they joined the steady stream of patrons heading to the lobby.

"It's an interesting production, though I am not generally one for plays and novels."

"Indeed? Then where do your interests lie?"

They had made their way to the lobby and were able to step outside into the cool night air. Fianna appeared to be thinking over his question. Had no one ever asked her about herself?

"I suppose I enjoy what most young ladies do when they are preparing for marriage," she said after a time. "I spend a great deal of time learning about running a household."

The sorts of activities Fletcher's mother would expect of his wife.

"Surely you must have other hobbies?" Fletcher asked. He wasn't sure why he was pushing, whether it was for her benefit or his own. "Things you do for your own enjoyment?"

Fianna opened her mouth, then closed it again. "Is that important?"

Very, Fletcher thought to himself. How could he be expected to spend his entire life with someone and not know such a basic thing about them.

"I think the intermission is just about to end, we should go back in."

"Of course." Fianna took his arm and they headed inside. Once seated in the box, Fletcher noted that everyone was present except for his mother. He didn't get much time to dwell on the fact before the curtain rose.

CHAPTER EIGHTEEN

Some curtain calls were more anticipated than others and Adelia had to admit to herself that this was one evening she was relieved to take a bow.

Despite her best efforts she'd found her mind wandering to the theater box where she knew Fletcher was seated with his mother and the woman his mother wanted him to marry.

She couldn't help but wonder what Fletcher was thinking as he watched the play. Was he comparing her to the lady at his side? Even if he was, Adelia knew that it didn't matter. As an actress she would always be considered vulgar.

They were colleagues. Perhaps friends. They couldn't possibly be anything more.

"Excellent performance," Renata called from backstage as Adelia headed to the dressing rooms.

Adelia nodded her thanks, but she didn't feel as though the praise were deserved. Her mind hadn't been completely on her performance. Though, she supposed thinking about a man wasn't too far off the character of Miranda.

It was with that thought that she consoled herself as she arrived at her dressing room, where she found Beulah wringing her hands outside the door.

"There's a lady to see you," Beulah said in a low voice.

"Where?" Adelia asked, not understanding the other woman's distress.

"In there." Beulah nodded at the door.

"You let a stranger into my dressing room?"

"She wasn't the kind of lady you could say no to, Miss."

"I don't suppose you got a name?"

Beulah shook her head as she backed away from the door. "If it's all the same to you, Miss, you can ring me when she's gone and I'll come back to help you change."

Not waiting for Adelia's reply, Beulah was hurrying backstage.

Adelia couldn't think of who would be waiting for her. Visitors after a show were nothing new, but no one ever entered her dressing room without permission and certainly not before she'd had a chance to change out of her costume.

Thinking she would make quick work of the meeting, Adelia opened her dressing room door and stopped short.

The haughty woman who sat on her settee was a stranger to her, though Adelia had a nagging sensation that there was something familiar about her.

She was middle aged, dressed in navy blue silk. Her hair was pulled back into an elegant chignon and had a few traces of gray. But it was her eyes that drew Adelia in.

They were a familiar shade of hazel.

Which was when Adelia realized exactly who the woman was.

Of course, while she'd been busy trying to figure out who was in her dressing room, Lady Fletchingham had also been doing her own observing, making Adelia fully aware that she was still in costume with her hair half down in a Renaissance style.

"Have we met?" Adelia asked, finally finding her voice.

"No, but we have a mutual acquaintance in my son."

"And you're here on his behalf?" Even as she asked the question, Adelia knew it couldn't be the truth.

Lady Fletchingham straightened in her seat and puffed out her chest. While she had many physical traits in common with her son, she lacked warmth. And while Fletcher kept his true feeling under wraps, he was never cold. "My son is an eminently eligible bachelor. I make it my business to get involved when I feel he is losing sight of his responsibilities."

"Your son is a grown man," Adelia said, stepping out of the doorway and into her dressing room. Fletcher's mother might be a force to be reckoned with, but it wasn't like Adelia hadn't faced her fair share of dragons. At least she had on stage.

"My son has obviously been turned by a pretty face. He is neglecting his duties to his family and I am here to remind him to be a better man."

Adelia knew Lady Fletchingham's words were meant as a put down, to embarrass her. But the emotion that bubbled to the surface was anger.

She walked across the room and sat at the chair in front of her dressing table.

"This is a conversation you should be having with your son. It's clear to me that if you believe him to be neglecting his duties to his family then perhaps you do not know him particularly well after all."

Adelia turned her back on the woman, though she could still see her outraged face reflected in her mirror and reached for a brush to give her hands something to do. There was a slight tremor in her fingers and she wasn't certain if it was from anger or nerves. Likely a combination of the two.

"I should have known better than to expect manners from a common actress. But let me be perfectly clear. My son's fortune will not be at your disposal. You should keep that in mind and move on to your next benefactor."

Adelia met Lady Fletchingham's flinty stare through the mirror. "Perhaps you feel that your son's fortune is his only virtue, but I can assure you he has many other fine attributes to recommend him."

She hadn't thought it possible for the woman to puff up any further, but Adelia had been mistaken.

"I will not be spoken to like this. Not by a gutter—"

"Then I suggest you leave my dressing room," Adelia said, her knuckles turning white from her tight grip on the brush.

"I'll leave when I'm ready."

"No Mother, you'll leave now."

Adelia turned around to face the doorway where Fletcher stood, eyes on his mother. The expression he wore was one Adelia had never seen before. His eyes flashed with flecks of green and his lips formed a tight line. Where his mother was ice, Fletcher's anger was fire.

"You'll take the side of a trollop over your own mother?" Lady Fletchingham stood up. Yet, while her appearance had initially been crisp and impressive, Adelia saw signs of wilting.

"You should never have come here." Fletcher's voice was steady, but there was a roughness, like he was trying to keep from boiling over. "We'll discuss it later."

"We'll discuss it now while you escort me back up to your guests."

"I'll join you momentarily. You found your way down here on your own, I imagine you can find the way back out."

With a glare in Adelia's direction, Lady Fletchingham swept out of the room. Fletcher walked over to the dressing table, crouching in front of her chair. His eyes hadn't fully lost their spark, but there was no anger in his expression.

"I'm sorry for that. I had no idea my mother was down here."

"You don't have to apologize. Her words didn't affect me."

Fletcher reached out, lightly touching the hand that gripped the brush.

"Are you certain?"

She released the brush, laying it on her dressing table. "I appreciate the apology, but you did nothing wrong."

"All the same, I feel responsible. It's becoming remarkably apparent that I have not been nearly forthright enough where my mother is concerned." Fletcher straightened. "I'll leave you to change for the evening while I say my goodbyes to my mother's guests. I'll meet you in the lobby when you are ready."

"I can find another escort for the evening."

"I'm sure you could," Fletcher said, heading to the door. "Take your time and I'll meet you in the lobby."

I can assure you he has many other fine attributes to recommend him.

The words he'd overheard Adelia say to his mother played over and over in his head, filling him with a sense of pride.

Of course, under the circumstances he should be feeling nothing but anger and shame at his mother's actions.

True to his word, he'd returned to the theater box and escorted his mother and her guests to their carriages. His refusal to accompany them back to the hotel was met with hostility from the countess, but he saw a rare crack in his mother's armor in the wary expression she gave him as the door on her carriage closed.

They were due a difficult conversation but now wasn't the time to have it.

Instead he went back to the lobby where the crowd had thinned out considerably. Adelia did not keep him waiting long. She arrived wearing a dress of deep blue silk. It was a good color for her, but not as eye-catching as her usual red evening gowns. Not that Adelia could ever blend in.

"I hope you haven't been waiting long?" She asked.

Fletcher was glad to see that she looked calmer now.

In her dressing room, her cheeks had been flushed and he wasn't certain if she was holding back embarrassment or anger. He hoped it was the latter. The only person who deserved to feel shame was his mother.

"Not at all. If you are ready?"

Fletcher offered his arm and Adelia took it, though he noted her fingers barely grazed the cloth of his coat. Perhaps she was still upset over the things his mother had said. They'd talk about it later, after they'd made their rounds in the green room.

The usual crowd of actors and their companions were already there. Fletcher took Adelia straight to Davis.

"Just who I wanted to see!" Davis said, patting Fletcher on the shoulder. "It will please you to know that everyone I've asked has been enthusiastically in favor of participating in the recitations and I've secured rooms for us at the inn in Briarwood—at your recommendation."

"And you reached out to the bookshop?" Fletcher asked.

"I did and the owner is more than ready to sponsor the event. I must say, it's a fabulous idea. We'll get an afternoon at the races out of it too."

"As always I appreciate your enthusiasm," Fletcher said. "And I believe we are looking forward to a few days of fun, aren't we Adelia dear?"

"Yes, of course," Adelia agreed. "I'm certain it will be the culminating event in what has already been an exciting trip."

Though her words indicated her interest, Fletcher could see that something of her usual spark had dulled. Though never overly emotive in public, there were little tells that gave away her interest in her surroundings—the brightness in her eyes, the tilt of her head, the way she cocked an eyebrow when something caught her attention. But tonight there was no keenness behind the mask. She was simply going through the motions. He cursed his mother yet again for interfering.

They made their rounds, but Davis was really the only person Fletcher had needed to speak to, everyone else was just a necessary part of keeping up appearances. When he suggested they leave early, Adelia readily agreed.

Fletcher ordered a carriage. It wasn't a particularly cold night but a heavy mist hung in the air. The drive was silent and it reminded Fletcher of their first carriage ride, back in London. Had it really only been mere weeks that they'd been in each other's company? It felt like she'd been in his life much longer. How on earth was he going to resume his normal life without seeing her everyday?

And what kind of ridiculous thought was that?

The carriage came to a stop in front of their hotel and Fletcher helped Adelia descend. They climbed the stairs in silence and entered their drawing room. As they'd been told not to wait up, neither Myles nor Lilah were there to greet them.

"It has been a long day," Adelia said, not meeting Fletcher's eye. "If it's all the same, I'm going to turn in now."

"Wait." Fletcher reached for her hand and while she still didn't meet his gaze, she didn't pull away from him. "I know my mother upset you and I will be speaking to her about it. You won't have to see her again."

"Your mother didn't upset me. She merely reminded

me of the truth. That our arrangement is temporary."

Adelia finally glanced up at him and Fletcher saw that what she'd been fighting to conceal all night hadn't been anger—it had been sadness.

"Our friendship doesn't have to end," Fletcher said, the words rushing out.

She took in a sharp breath. "Of course it does. You can't be seen with an actress when you're married to a proper lady."

"Then I won't marry a proper lady."

Adelia's lips pulled at the corners, but it wasn't enough to make her truly smile. "You will marry, and sooner rather than later. Your mother won't rest until you do."

She squeezed his fingers before pulling out of his grasp and heading to her rooms. As the door gently closed behind her, Fletcher felt a terrible tightness in his chest, like he'd suffered the loss of something precious that he hadn't realized was within his grasp.

CHAPTER NINETEEN

The second expedition to Briarwood was very different from their first. Mainly because Mr. Davis had insisted on arranging—and therefore accompanying them—in their conveyance.

Their carriage was one of half a dozen that made up a convoy heading out of Belfast. Those behind them were filled with her fellow actors whom she believed were travelling in much tighter quarters.

Adelia had a book open on her lap, but found she'd barely read a page. Though Mr. Davis kept his conversation mainly to Fletcher, she still half listened.

"The races in England have nothing on the ones here in Ireland," Mr. Davis explained. "The quality of horses simply cannot be matched."

Though Fletcher appeared to be looking at Mr. Davis, and even listening, Adelia saw that he was tapping his pointer finger against his right knee—a sign that he was lost in thought.

Adelia looked out the window while Mr. Davis went off on a tangent about horse breeding. Though she'd seen this particular countryside not that long ago, Adelia enjoyed watching the trees and villages. Having spent her life in the city, any sign of country life was of particular interest.

She'd spent the days leading up to what had become known as "Race Day" in practicing recitations and helping the other actors, many of whom had never had many lines before, prepare monologues. She'd kept herself so busy that she'd hardly spent any time in Fletcher's company since the night of his mother's arrival in her dressing room. She'd come to the horrible realization, after speaking with Lady Fletchingham, that she actually enjoyed Fletcher's presence in her life, a circumstance she had to remedy because there was no way for their friendship to continue when they returned to London. Therefore, her plan had been to wean herself off Fletcher's company.

Of course, once she'd gotten into the carriage and sat next to him, her plan had flown out the window.

They came upon a village that Adelia remembered from a few days before with a stone inn and a large courtyard. She'd been particularly struck by the early blooming rose bushes, though this time much of the garden was obstructed by the presence of an enormous carriage being pulled by four horses.

"Whose carriage is that?" Adelia asked and Mr. Davis stopped in the middle of a sentence to look out his window.

"Oh, that's the Morrissey's eight-seater."

Adelia stiffened but Fletcher leaned in close, speaking in a low voice. "We fully expected James to come to the races."

Mr. Davis seemed not to notice their exchange and

launched back into his own conversation, having moved on from horses to talk about the arena itself.

"There's nothing like it in England—it's absolutely state of the art."

"Yes well, we've been somewhat hampered by war debt," Fletcher muttered, but yet again Mr. Davis seemed so focused on his own stories that he didn't hear anyone else.

Adelia leaned forward in time to see the grand carriage pull away from the inn and force its way onto the road behind them.

Whether it was the stress of seeing the Morrisseys or the stress of trying to keep an emotional distance from Fletcher, Adelia could feel the beginnings of a headache. She absently rubbed at her temple. The action wasn't lost on Fletcher.

"Are you quite all right?"

Adelia nodded absently. "It's just a headache."

"We should pull over," Fletcher said to Mr. Davis. "I think Adelia could use some air."

"Since we just passed an inn, it will likely be some time before we happen upon another," Mr. Davis said.

"Then I suggest you find an alternative," Fletcher said.

Mr. Davis stuck his head out the window, sizing up their surroundings while Adelia focused on her breathing. She knew Fletcher suspected she was about to have an episode, but that couldn't possibly be right. She knew for a fact she'd taken her blocker that morning. Still, she couldn't ignore the tingling sensation in her forehead.

Adelia leaned her head against the side of the carriage, closing her eyes. She focussed on her breathing.

"We need to stop now," she heard Fletcher say, though his voice sounded far off. There was a rapping against the ceiling of the carriage followed by a slowing of the horses. Finally they came to a stop and she felt fresh air pouring in.

"Come," Fletcher said, pulling her gently by the elbow. By the time she'd descended the stairs he was half carrying her and she was only vaguely aware that they were surrounded by trees.

The tingling intensified and her vision blurred completely, replaced by the interior of another carriage. There was a man across from her with a lilting accent.

"Are you pleased with your conveyance?" The man asked, looking her over.

"I wouldn't have minded traveling with the others," her voice was pitched slightly higher.

"But you deserve the best, or at least the best I can give you."

She looked down at her hands, folded in her lap over her lavender skirts. "You're too good to me."

The man leaned forward, placing a finger under her chin and tipping her head up so that she looked into his deep green eyes. "For what you can give me, you're worth it."

The vision fell away and Adelia blinked rapidly, clearing her eyes. She and Fletcher were hidden in the trees, a few feet away from the road. He had his hands on her upper arms, holding her up. He leaned down to look into her face. This close she could see that his hazel eyes had gone deep brown.

"Are you all right?"

Adelia nodded, not trusting herself to speak when Fletcher's lips were mere inches from her own. He straightened but didn't release her.

"We'll tell Davis you have carriage illness."

"That's good thinking," Adelia said, her voice coming out husky. She cleared her throat. "I'm ready to go back if you are."

"Can I ask if you saw anything of interest?"

Adelia thought back on the vision. Brief as it was, she knew exactly whose perspective she'd seen from.

"No, not this time."

The rest of the voyage continued without further incident, though Fletcher did notice that Davis gave Adelia strange, assessing looks when he thought he wasn't being watched.

As they pulled up to the inn, Fletcher was relieved to see that Morrissey's carriage continued on past. At least Fletcher wouldn't have to worry about running into him or his entourage at breakfast.

The innkeeper came out to the courtyard, eagerly awaiting their arrival.

"If you're ready, my wife will show you right to your room," the innkeeper said as a tall woman in an apron stepped forward to greet them. Given that they weren't used to an inn full of guests, Fletcher was glad for their enthusiasm.

"If you'll follow me," the innkeeper's wife said, leading them into the foyer and up a set of stairs. She opened the door with a hopeful smile. "This is our finest suite."

Adelia stepped into the small, but neat, sitting room. The walls and furniture were shades of blue and green that matched the seaview out the picture window.

"It's charming," she said, returning the woman's smile. "Are the bedrooms through there?"

"Just the one bedroom," the woman said, her smile faltering slightly. "Will that be a problem?"

"Not at all," Fletcher said, stepping fully into the room. "This is a most charming suite."

"I'll have your bags sent straight up along with some tea," the woman said with a quick curtsy. As she closed the door behind her, Adelia turned to Fletcher.

"One bedroom?"

"Did you want me to blow our cover by asking for my own room?"

"You could have said it was because you snored." Adelia moved to the window. The view really was spectacular.

"Don't worry, I'll sleep out here."

Adelia looked away from the window to take in the light blue settee.

"That doesn't look particularly comfortable."

A smile tugged at the corners of his lips. "I've made do with worse, I assure you."

There was a knock on their door and Myles and Lilah entered with all their bags, Myles carrying the heavier items.

"We have rooms just down the hall," Lilah said, eyeing the one doorway off the sitting room. "Are the bedrooms through there?"

"It's just the one bedroom," Adelia said. "So we'll have

to take turns dressing."

"I can get ready with Myles," Fletcher said, turning to his valet. "Bring my bags to your room."

Myles hesitated. "It'll be a tight squeeze."

"I believe we'll manage."

As Lilah went through to the bedroom and Myles huffed his way down the hall, a tea tray arrived and they settled in the seating area. Adelia filled a cup and handed it to Fletcher.

"What's our plan going forward?"

Fletcher took the tea, noting that she'd remembered he took it with just a little milk and plenty of sugar.

"We've got the ball this evening."

Of course, the ball. It had been talked about incessantly in the days leading up to their excursion, but Adelia hadn't paid much attention.

"I can't believe the town actually invited all the actors to a ball." Adelia sipped her tea.

"It's at an assembly hall," Fletcher said. "It's hardly a high *ton* event."

"No," Adelia's forehead creased in a frown, "I suppose it isn't."

Fletcher set down his cup. He could have kicked himself. He sounded like an absolute snob. "I misspoke. What I meant to say is that it isn't one of those stuffy parties thrown by old society dragons. This might actually be fun."

The frown faded from Adelia's face. "You think so?"

"I intend to enjoy myself, and you should too."

"We're here to work," Adelia pointed out. "Not dance."

Fletcher reached for an apple tart. "Is there some rule that we can't do both?"

"No, I suppose not."

"And it's not likely that we'll need to work this evening. The ladies aren't leaving until tomorrow."

"I suppose you're right," Adelia said, tugging on a lock of hair behind her ear. "But perhaps we should keep an eye out just in case they decided to move the girls tonight instead."

"Never worry, I've got Myles on it. If they so much as move a toe out of that big blue house, he'll sound the alarm."

"That gives me some comfort," Adelia said, wrinkling her nose. "I suppose I'll have to start getting ready soon."

"Is it such a chore to accompany me to a ball?"

Adelia broke into a true smile. "It's a sacrifice I'm willing to make."

CHAPTER TWENTY

Adelia turned her head from side to side in the mirror, looking at the updo Lilah had worked on for the last half hour. She'd managed to do a sweeping hairstyle that left several locks down one side of her neck.

"You've outdone yourself."

Lilah beamed. "You should let me show off my skills more often."

"Perhaps I will," Adelia said, giving herself a final once over. She'd picked out a sapphire silk with a square neckline trimmed in black lace. Lilah had picked out a red satin, but Adelia had insisted on blue.

Adelia stood up and went to the drawing room where Fletcher was sitting by the fire, reading a newspaper.

For a moment she just stood there, watching him do something so terribly ordinary. Her imagination took off and she could see them as any other couple, preparing for an evening out. What if he weren't a peer or if she weren't an actress? Would an easy life together be possible for them?

But they couldn't change the lives they'd been born to, and there was no point in picturing anything different.

Adelia stepped fully into the room, the sound of her footsteps catching Fletcher's attention and he looked up from the newspaper. For a moment he just stared at her before setting the paper down next to him.

"You're beautiful."

"It's Lilah's handiwork." She felt her cheeks warm both from the compliment and the heat in his gaze. She cleared her throat. "You don't look too bad yourself."

It was true. As Fletcher stood up Adelia took in his black evening clothes. By some twist of fate he'd worn a red waistcoat. She thought with a pang, had she dressed as she usually did, they would have matched.

The intensity ebbed out of Fletcher's gaze, though it wasn't quite replaced by the usual easygoing mask he wore when out in public. Instead he looked at ease, almost relaxed.

"I suppose I should give Myles all the credit for my appearance, but in truth he did very little."

Adelia laughed. "I suppose that's fair, since men don't have to worry quite so much over their hairstyles."

Fletcher's gaze wandered from her updo, lingering on the locks that touched her neck, before resting on her face. Once again she knew her cheeks flushed under his observation.

"Shall we go?"

Fletcher offered his arm and they headed back down to the foyer where they were to meet Mr. Davis' carriage.

"It's such a short distance," Adelia said, "I feel we'll spend more time just getting into and out of the carriage."

"It's a nice evening, we could walk if you like?"

"But won't Mr. Davis be expecting us?"

"I'll leave a message with the innkeeper."

Fletcher went to find the innkeeper, Adelia waited for him near the check-in desk. She heard a crowd in the nearby dining room and stepped closer to see it was a familiar group of actors and the friends who'd come with them.

She saw Renata smiling at Calen and she was reminded again of the vision she'd had earlier in the day. Calen was a charming man, but she hoped Renata was taking care with her feelings. Adelia didn't want to see her friend hurt when they returned to London.

"You look delightful this evening."

Adelia turned to see Bertie coming down the stairs. He stopped next to her, peering into the doorway, a scowl forming on his face.

"That's a development I don't like." He nodded at Calen and Renata.

"You think he'll break her heart?"

"Yes, but not in the way you're thinking. He's giving her delusions of grandeur, letting her believe she'll be the next great actress."

"Perhaps she will be."

"She's no Adelia Dumont."

Adelia playfully hit her friend in the arm. "Are you coming to the ball?"

"Save me from society affairs," Bertie said. "I'm going to enjoy my evening off."

"I'll see you at the races then?"

"Wouldn't miss it." Bertie gave her a quick peck on the cheek and headed into the dining room.

"Are you ready?"

Adelia turned around to see Fletcher standing behind her.

He looked past her into the dining room, his gaze falling on Bertie. "Unless you wanted to speak to your friends first?"

"No, I'm ready."

"Shall we then?" Fletcher held his arm out and Adelia placed her hand on his elbow and they walked out the door.

The night air was pleasantly cool, but not so much so that she needed more than a shawl. Again, Adelia was struck by how natural it felt to stroll with Fletcher. She was going to miss having him as an escort.

"Dare I ask what has you so lost in thought?" Fletcher asked as they passed the now closed bookstore.

"I was just thinking about how odd it will feel to go back to normal life after all this."

"You mean the travel? Or the mission?"

She paused for a minute. "I think I mean both."

"Will you have a break, or do you already have your next project lined up?"

"Mr. Davis is planning *Much Ado About Nothing* for the summer season. I have been offered the part of Beatrice if I'd like it."

"You don't want to take some time off?"

Adelia shrugged. "I wouldn't know what to do with myself."

"Perhaps an escape to the country?"

"Perhaps. Though, what I would very much like to do is direct a play."

As soon as the words were out of her mouth, Adelia

wondered what had possessed her to share one of her biggest secrets.

"Really?" Fletcher brought them to a stop. Adelia waited for him to laugh at the idea of a woman directing but instead he nodded slowly. "I think I'd like to see it."

"Well, you'd be the only one."

"I sincerely doubt that." The sun had set but, the rays still lit up the sky enough that Adelia could see Fletcher's eyes on her. He reached out, pulling on a lock of hair that rested against her shoulder. "You're an extraordinary woman, you know that?"

Adelia wasn't sure what to say, but words were unnecessary as Fletcher leaned forward and ever so briefly touched his lips to hers.

"Shall we continue on?" Fletcher asked. Adelia nodded dumbly, completely at a loss for words.

Normally Fletcher didn't pay much attention to the details of a ball. He didn't care about flowers, or guest lists. Usually he did his best to disappear into one of the games rooms. But on this particular evening he stayed in the main ballroom, playing dutiful escort.

And he found he was having more fun than he'd ever thought possible at a ball. The assembly rooms in Briarwood were so rarely used that a ball attracted guests from two resorts over, making the event a veritable squeeze.

Despite her misgivings, Adelia fit in splendidly. He'd led her out in the first set of dances and then had watched while she was swept up for the second set by Mr. Davis. Once the dance was finished, Adelia returned to him, her cheeks pink from exertion.

"I forgot how much I liked to dance," she said, watching as couples lined up once again.

Fletcher frowned. "Don't you get many opportunities to dance?"

Adelia shook her head. "I don't go to many balls."

"Would you like to dance again?"

"With you? Isn't it poor taste since we just danced the first set?"

"I doubt anyone here would care."

Adelia fanned her face. "Perhaps later. I think I'd like some refreshment first."

"Indeed? Then lead the way."

Adelia quirked a brow and held her elbow out, mimicking Fletcher's stance when they walked together. Laughter burst from his lips causing more than one head to turn their way. He ignored them and daintily placed his hand on her elbow. Adelia's lips split into a wide smile.

"Lord Fletchingham?"

Fletcher dropped his hand as he turned around to find himself face to face with Lady Fianna. She was dressed in a blush colored gown and a jeweled headband that looked out of place in the country ballroom.

In fact, everything about Lady Fianna felt out of place.

"What are you doing here?" He knew it was a rude question, but he'd been caught off guard.

"I'm here with my mother and Lady Fletchingham. The ambassador invited us to be his guests for the races tomorrow."

As Fianna spoke she was joined by her mother.

"How pleasant," Countess Sinclair's keen gaze flickered between Fletcher and Adelia, "when we heard about a ball in Briarwood, your dear mama was certain you'd be here this evening."

"Well you have the advantage of me," Fletcher said.

"Oh!" Fianna held her gloved hand up to her mouth. "Is that Adelia Dumont with you?"

Fletcher glanced to where Adelia had been standing next to him to find that she'd taken a few steps back, apparently trying to blend into a nearby crowd.

Which was ridiculous. She was an invited guest just like everyone else.

"Yes, it is," Fletcher said, taking Adelia by the elbow and pulling her to his side. "Miss Dumont, this is Lady Fianna and the Countess Sinclair."

"A pleasure," the countess said through a thin-lipped smile.

Fletcher could feel Adelia's arm stiffen where he held her elbow and he knew if given the choice she would flee. Yet he couldn't let her go.

"Now that we've found you," Countess Sinclair continued speaking, though her gaze was on the point where Adelia's arm was linked through Fletcher's, "I assume you will want to have the next dance with Fianna. I am sure your companion won't mind."

"I'm sure she would," Fletcher said. "I'm truly sorry, Lady Fianna, but I have just promised to bring Adelia to the supper room. You will excuse us?"

Fletcher didn't wait for an answer. Instead he turned his back to the countess and led Adelia around the edge of the dance floor.

"What are you doing?" Adelia's voice was barely above a whisper. "You can't just walk away from a countess."

"I was raised with better manners than to drop one lady at the arrival of another."

"I would have been fine. Besides, I'm not a lady."

Fletcher stopped, bringing Adelia to a halt next to him. His temper, never far from the surface when there was evidence of his mother's meddling, bubbled over.

"You're a lady if I say you are."

Adelia's eyes darted toward the dance floor, then back to Fletcher. "We're being watched."

Fletcher forced the anger down. The last thing he wanted was for anyone to think he was angry with the woman at his side.

"Then let's get to the supper room and get you fed."

CHAPTER TWENTY-ONE

"Is it safe?" Adelia asked in a quiet voice as Lilah crept back into the bedroom of her suite.

"Yes, Miss, he's still asleep on the couch."

"He didn't stir when you walked past?"

"No, Miss."

Adelia nodded at her maid's words. Though they hadn't gotten home until late into the night, she'd had a hard time falling asleep and had woken early. Her nerves were shot and she knew it had nothing to do with her recitation later that evening and everything to do with the mission. And possibly also a little to do with Fletcher.

Actually, it had a lot to do with Fletcher.

What on earth had he been doing the night before? Going up against a countess and her daughter? A daughter who absolutely had to be one of Fletcher's marriage prospects.

Adelia had never felt so on display in her life—despite the fact she worked on stage.

But the thing that weighed her down wasn't just Fletcher's actions toward the countess. It was also his actions toward herself. He was kind, considerate, and genuinely seemed to enjoy her company.

And why did that bother her so much?

Was it because no matter what either of them felt, they had no future together? All they had was this one mission that was quickly coming to an end.

Adelia paused on her way to the bedroom door, catching sight of herself in the mirror. She'd gone ahead and dressed for the races, wearing a fuschia day dress that not only stood out, but was also dark enough that even if she got swept up by a crowd, any dirt or stains wouldn't easily show through.

Moving with care, she slowly opened the door to her bedroom and crept into the sitting room. Almost of their own volition, her eyes moved to the chaise where Fletcher was stretched out, his feet hanging over the end. He was still in the trousers and waistcoat from the night before, but the jacket and cravat had been discarded over a nearby chair. Several shirt buttons had been left undone, revealing a few inches of tanned chest.

Adelia swallowed hard. She was staring.

Giving herself a mental shake, she headed past the settee toward the door.

"You don't need to go looking for breakfast, it will be here soon."

Adelia jerked in surprise and turned back toward the settee. Fletcher hadn't moved, but his hazel eyes were focused on her.

"I was going to go for a walk."

Fletcher sat up, swinging his stocking feet around to rest on the floor. "You can't go out without breakfast first."

"Yes I can."

But Fletcher shook his head. "Come sit. We need to talk."

Adelia glanced at the door where she'd almost escaped and, with a sigh, went to sit in the wingback chair closest to the settee because the other was covered in Fletcher's clothes.

"What do we need to talk about?"

There was a knock on the door and Fletcher called out, inviting a kitchen maid in with a tray. Rather than setting it up on the table by the window, Fletcher directed her to the coffee table in front of him.

Once the maid left, he poured two cups of tea.

"Unfortunately they don't have coffee here," Fletcher said, handing a cup to Adelia. It had a little sugar and no milk, just like she always drank it. She took a sip before setting it aside. There was no way she could drink the tea with her stomach churning. Whatever Fletcher wanted to talk to her about, it couldn't be good.

She watched him, waiting for him to speak but he hesitated, running a hand through his hair, leaving it slightly mussier than usual.

He likely wanted to make sure they were both on the same page going forward. They'd shared another kiss last night and now he needed reassurance that there wouldn't be any complications when he went back to London and married his perfect, well-bred bride.

Seeing Fletcher's difficulty in getting the conversation started, Adelia made up her mind to clear the air.

"I know what you want to talk about," she said.

Fletcher raised a brow. "You think so?"

"Yes. And I want to assure you that I will do everything I can to ease the rumors on my end so that when we return to London you can marry with ease."

"That's what you think I want to talk to you about?"

"Yes."

Fletcher shook his head and picked up his teacup, putting it down without taking a sip. "Do we have anything stronger here?"

"It's morning."

He leaned forward, resting his elbows on his knees. "You know that normally if a gentleman and a lady spend an evening together in a suite like this, the lady should expect a marriage proposal?"

"Fortunately for you, I'm not a lady."

"And this is why I wanted a drink," Fletcher muttered to himself getting to his feet.

"What are you doing?" Adelia asked, twisting in her chair so she could see Fletcher head toward a cabinet.

"I'm trying to propose to you, but since you're making it remarkably difficult I need a drink."

"I'm sorry, you're doing what?"

Fletcher found a bottle and returned to the settee. He popped open the bottle of brandy and poured a measure into his tea. Adelia held up her own cup. "If you could add just a little, if you please."

Fletcher did as she asked and sat down, leaving the bottle between them. For a moment, neither of them spoke. Adelia took tiny sips from her tea, but it still burned her throat on the way down.

"Well?" Fletcher finally asked. "What do you think?"

"What do I think of what?" Adelia repeated.

"My proposal."

"I don't understand it. Do you want me to become your mistress?"

Fletcher set his cup down with a thunk. "That's not what I asked."

"Then what? We can't marry."

"Why not? Men and women do it all the time."

"Perhaps they do. But not men like you and women like me."

"You mean because I have a title?"

"And I'm an actress."

Fletcher's lips formed a thin line. "I had noticed."

At that moment the door opened and Myles walked into the room. He paused when he saw Fletcher and Adelia.

"Apologies, I thought you were still asleep, my lord. I was just coming to tell you it's time to get ready."

"Of course it is." Fletcher drained his cup as he stood up. He looked at Adelia. "We'll continue this conversation later."

"Unless you come to your senses," Adelia muttered to herself, picking up her tea.

Fletcher felt lighter.

Adelia might not have given him a proper answer, but she hadn't seemed repulsed by his proposal.

No, she'd been focused on the differences in their backgrounds, but she hadn't said she didn't care for him.

Once they got through the day— and more importantly their mission that evening— he'd approach the topic again. If she was hesitant about being accepted into his social circle, they could take their time until she became more comfortable. And if anyone snubbed her, it wouldn't bother him in the least to cut out some of the snobs his mother considered close friends. It would allow them more evenings to sit at home reading in peace.

Since Adelia had already dressed, they left the inn as soon as Fletcher was ready, taking a carriage to the arena. Unfortunately, Davis joined them, making it impossible to continue their conversation from earlier.

"We're coming up on the arena," Davis said. Since he was sitting with his back to the horses, he had to twist his upper body around to see out the window, effectively blocking Fletcher's view. Adelia had no such obstructions and whatever she could see out of her side of the carriage had her complete attention.

"It's the largest race track in Europe," Davis continued. "The interior seats a thousand spectators."

"A thousand?" Adelia asked, not taking her eyes off the view out her window. "How on earth can so many people fit into one space together?"

"Well, you won't see even half that many today. The National Stakes is an elite race—invitation only. There will be no vulgar crowds, I assure you."

The last part of Davis' statement was directed at Fletcher and while he wanted to tell the other man that he was capable of putting up with much more than a 'vulgar crowd' Davis chose that moment to move out of the way, thus giving Fletcher his first proper view of the arena.

Built in a valley between two cliffs overlooking the ocean, the arena stuck out from its surroundings like a jewel on a beach. A massive jewel.

The building was oval-shaped and the exterior was painted in shades of red, green and gold. As they drew closer, Fletcher could see arches all the way around, though there were no actual windows. Instead there was a massive canopy over a set of double doors indicating the main entrance.

They pulled into a line of carriages and crept along. Davis continued prattling on, though neither Fletcher nor Adelia responded to him. He finally stopped speaking when they rolled up to the awning. Fletcher descended from the carriage, holding a hand out to Adelia who seemed quite taken by the pattern on the canopy over their heads. On closer inspection, Fletcher could see that it was covered in a pattern of gold shamrocks.

Adelia tucked her arm into Fletcher's elbow, but her eyes were on their surroundings. He couldn't blame her. Once they stepped inside, there was a large foyer with hallways veering off in opposite directions.

"The left leads to the boxes," Davis said. "But we'll be going to the right, as you requested, my lord."

Adelia gave him a curious look. "You aren't sitting in a box?"

Fletcher grinned. "Not today."

They fell into line with the other patrons, though Fletcher noticed the discomfort on Davis' face at being so close to the masses. Fletcher had no such concerns.

The line moved quickly and they were soon within view of the stands.

"Oh my!" Adelia's voice came out as a whisper.

In front of them was seating for hundreds of people,

though there were only dozens, scattered about in the front rows.

Then there was the track itself. Fletcher couldn't imagine how a ring of red dirt could look so glorious. It was just over a mile around and in the center was a green section with a wooden stage from where the announcer would speak. The stage was ringed in garlands of red roses. A massive gong sat in the grass on the right corner of the stage and while there were no windows around the arena, a skylight in the roof lit up the race track, letting in natural light.

"Where are we sitting?" Adelia asked, giving his arm a light squeeze.

"Do you see that line of white in the dirt?" Fletcher pointed to the end of the oval. "That's the finish line. Our seats are right in front of it."

"We'll be right next to the horses?"

"If that suits you? It's not too late to go to a box."

Her eyes lit up as she looked at him and though they were in a public place, surrounded by people, she didn't bother hiding her excitement. "I want to sit in the stands."

On their way to the seats, Fletcher stopped an usher and picked up a program of the day's races. They followed Davis toward their seats, though Fletcher noted the man moved with a stiffness.

"Perhaps you can hand me the tickets?" Fletcher asked. "While you secure a box in the event we feel the need to retire to a more civilized environment?"

"Oh, yes!" Davis nodded immediately. "An excellent idea. I'll do that right away."

They watched Davis head off and Adelia turned to him with a smile.

"That was kind of you," she said.

"You think so?"

She nodded. "It was obvious that he was uncomfortable down here in the stands and you gave him an excuse to escape."

"Or perhaps I simply wanted to be alone with you." Fletcher watched in delight as Adelia's cheeks flushed.

He led her to a staircase and past the rows of empty stands until they reached the front row. While there were several clusters of people, the area around the seats Davis had secured for them were empty.

Adelia settled on the bench in front of a low fence. They were near enough to the track that Fletcher thought he could reach out and touch it.

"It smells like horses," Adelia said, wrinkling her nose.

"One of the hazards of our seats. There's still time to move to a box."

Adelia looked over her shoulder at the boxed seating that ringed the uppermost level of the arena.

"I don't think the view would be as good."

"You are correct," Fletcher said. "But perhaps we can do something about the smell."

He waved over a passing vendor and bought two ham and cheese pastries, handing one over to Adelia. "Perhaps the aroma of fresh pastries will help."

"Even if it doesn't, these are delicious," she said, sinking her teeth into the flaky crust. She looked around while chewing. "Do you think they ever fill all these seats?"

"I'm certain they do during the annual derby. That's open to everyone."

"It must be such a sight," Adelia said, looking around as though she were imagining all the seats were filled with people.

"Perhaps we'll come back for it." As he said the words, Fletcher was already thinking about what it would be like to travel with Adelia just because they could.

"Fletcher—"

"We'll discuss it later," he said. "Work first."

Adelia looked like she was about to argue with him again, but instead she went back to her pastry.

They finished just as a bearded man in an emerald green jacket walked up to the main stage. He stood beside a stand with a brass megaphone.

"He looks like a very tall leprechaun," Adelia whispered and Fletcher couldn't help but laugh.

"Ladies and gentlemen," the man's voice reverberated throughout the arena. "Welcome to the National Stakes. I know you are all here for the main event, but before we get started, we have a very special race."

The arena was filled with a screeching sound, like gears whirring, and Adelia and Fletcher looked around to see what was causing the noise.

"Are those steam carriages?" Adelia asked, her brow furrowing.

As the vehicles came further into view, Fletcher could see that unlike the carriages on the streets of London, these were open top.

"They can't run on aether," Fletcher said, sitting up fully. "It's against Irish law and besides, it would harm the horses."

"Ladies and gentlemen, what you are witnessing is the inaugural race between the first ever aether internalized engines!"

"That's not possible," Fletcher muttered to himself.

"An internalized engine? That means no aether fumes, right?" Adelia said.

Fletcher nodded, though his attention was still on the start line where two vehicles were taking their position. One was painted bright, cherry red, while the other was sky blue. On closer inspection, Fletcher could see that the carriages had three wheels instead of four and were only large enough to seat a driver.

"This is remarkable," Adelia said. She was leaning forward, gloved hands gripping the top of the fence so she could have a better view.

"It's impossible," Fletcher said. "As far as the British government knows, this technology doesn't exist."

Up on stage, the master of ceremonies stepped away from the megaphone and nodded toward a man standing in the grass in front of the stage near the gong. The man held up a mallet and hit the center of the brass disk. At the sound, there was a whirring and growling from the other end of the arena.

Adelia tried to say something, but though Fletcher could see her lips move, he couldn't hear her words. Their attention, like that of everyone else in the arena, was drawn to the race oval where the two horseless carriages barrelled down the track.

Fletcher couldn't be certain, but he didn't think they were travelling faster than a good thoroughbred. Still, the fact this engine existed was extraordinary.

They watched as the blue carriage led the whole way around the track, only to be overtaken at the last moment by the red.

"How extraordinary," Adelia said, clapping her gloved hands along with everyone else.

Fletcher reached into his inside jacket pocket and took out a notebook and small pencil and made a few notes for later. He needed to figure out the origin of that engine. He doubted it could be Irish, they had too many contacts in the country for such an invention to fall through the cracks.

Several men came out with rakes to fix up the track and Adelia looked around the stadium while Fletcher finished up his notes.

"Your mother is here," Adelia said, a frown line between her eyebrows. "She's in a box directly behind us."

"She must be here with the ambassador." Fletcher put the notebook back in his pocket. Unlike Adelia he didn't feel the need to turn around to see his mother. He could already picture the expression on her face.

"Don't worry about her," Fletcher said, taking Adelia's gloved hand in an attempt to draw her attention away from the boxes. "See? They're bringing the horses out."

CHAPTER TWENTY-TWO

Fletcher may have been able to ignore his mother's presence but Adelia could not. She could feel the woman's eyes boring into the back of her head.

The horse race had been every bit as exciting as she'd thought it would be. Sitting where they were, they'd been nearly within arm's reach of the fabulous animals as they'd run past to the finish line.

"There's a tea back at the inn in Briarwood. We should make an appearance," Fletcher said after the winners had been crowned in the center of the arena.

"I need time to prepare for this evening."

Adelia's monologues, and the crowd coming and going to see her, would hopefully provide the necessary distraction for Fletcher's team to intercept the vessel that was due to take the women away.

"I know you have your lines completely memorized. You can take a little time to have tea with your friends."

Adelia had to admit that she felt strangely at home at the inn and she knew the other actors would be at the inn.

"You're right," Adelia said.

"Those words sound good leaving your lips," Fletcher said with a wink.

"Don't get used to hearing them."

Fletcher managed to get a separate carriage from Mr. Davis for the trip back, which allowed them to be alone for the first time since that morning. Adelia found that she both desperately wanted to ask about his marriage proposal and also never once bring it up again.

It didn't matter though, they had too much to discuss regarding their mission, allowing Adelia to push the thoughts to one side.

"Myles will await the signal from the airship offshore," Fletcher started. "It's important that I make an appearance at your show this evening, but once I do, I'll go back to Myles to assist where needed. Based on what we've been able to find around the docks, we believe the women will be ferried out in one dory, which will mean they'll need to make several trips, assuming Captain Cartright is correct in his estimation of the number of women he's seen from the institute."

"We'll need to get one of our men driving the dory?" Adelia asked.

"Yes. That should be a relatively easy task for Myles. He'll incapacitate Jackson's man so one of ours can take over. If everything goes as planned, we'll have diverted the women to our ship before anyone realizes what's happening."

"And it's really an airship that's coming?"

"Meri's latest correspondence indicates that there'll be a ship landing in the harbor just after sunset. There will be a small crew of agents to help us but we're trying to keep their arrival as unremarkable as possible."

"Do you think it's possible for an airship to go completely unnoticed?"

Fletcher shrugged. "I hope. It's a small ship and the pilot will be making a blind landing."

A blind landing was done with no light source and often required cutting the engines while still up in the sky to minimize noise. Adelia had never seen such a landing, but Meri had described them to her before when they'd discussed his training.

"Will Meri be landing the ship? I know he's occupied with naval duties."

"I think he was able to get away, just for the evening."

Adelia smiled as they bumped along the road. She put her hand out, grabbing onto the edge of the seat to catch herself from toppling forward.

"That's good then. Meri's the best."

Fletcher didn't return her smile. "You think so?"

Adelia had the impression she'd said something wrong. She tried to think what it was but the carriage slowed in front of the inn, cutting off their conversation.

The dining room of the Briarwood Inn had been transformed with all the tables pushed back to allow for a greater number of patrons to move through. To make the most of the space, there wasn't a formal dining area. Instead, the tables along the walls were laid out with pastries and sandwiches.

"Can I get you a plate?" Fletcher asked.

"Just a few things," Adelia said. "I don't usually eat much before a performance."

Fletcher gave her a nod. "I had noticed."

Adelia stood still, watching while he went off to the tables, replaying the last of their conversation in her head. All she'd done was bring up how competent Meri was. Surely this was something Fletcher already knew?

As he reached the table, Adelia saw that Fletcher's attention was taken by Mr. Davis. Knowing it could be ages before he was able to return to her side, she decided to go find some of her own people to talk to. There was a group milling outside in the gardens and there was an excellent view of the water.

Adelia was nearly to the French doors when a figure stepped in front of her, blocking her path. It took her a moment to realize she wasn't having a vision—such was her surprise at seeing the woman before her in the less than illustrious surroundings.

"Lady Fletchingham?" Adelia said. "I didn't realize you were here."

Indeed, she'd had no reason to expect Fletcher's mother to show up at an informal tea at an inn. Particularly one where common actors were in attendance. After seeing Lady Fletchingham earlier at the races, Adelia had assumed she was staying with the ambassador at one of the more illustrious resorts.

"I assure you, I am not here by choice. I came on business."

"Business?" Adelia repeated.

"Come outside with me."

Her need to avoid a scene in the dining room had her feet carrying her out the door even before Adelia fully realized what she was doing.

Once they were on the terrace, away from the doors, Lady Fletchingham turned to Adelia, sweeping her appearance from head to toe.

"That's an interesting color."

Adelia glanced down at her fuschia skirts, but didn't respond.

"I don't suppose I have to tell you why I felt compelled to speak to you again."

"Forgive me, my lady, I am at a loss as to why you are here."

"Your audacity knows no bounds, but what more could one expect from a common actress."

"You don't respect me because of my work?"

"I don't respect you because you don't know your place."

Adelia could hear the chatter of voices coming out through the French doors. She didn't think anyone was close enough to overhear their conversation, but she wasn't certain that even the presence of an audience would stop Lady Fletchingham from airing her grievances.

"I apologize for offending you," Adelia said, hoping she could encourage the other woman to end the conversation.

"I do not require your apologies. I require action."

"And what action would that be?"

"Leave my son alone."

Adelia could feel the beginnings of a headache. Fortunately it wasn't accompanied by the tingling sensation of an attack.

"Perhaps you should be having this conversation with him."

Lady Fletchingham puffed up like an angry peacock. "My conversations with my son are my business. I came to you merely to appeal to your sense of decency."

"I'm surprised you think I have one," Adelia said. She could tell by the way Lady Fletchingham was puffing up that she wasn't going to be done with her speech anytime soon. Adelia needed to make her escape. "If you'll excuse me, we'll have to continue this conversation at another time. I have to prepare for this evening."

She didn't wait for Lady Fletchingham's answer. She turned, sweeping back into the dining room, hoping her outer shell of polite detachment held despite the fact that her heart was beating out of control.

She didn't look back, but she was certain she could feel the other woman's eyes on her. Adelia had meant what she'd said though—she had every intention of leaving the inn and heading to the assembly rooms to prepare for the evening. She was so intent on making her escape, that she very nearly walked into Renata.

"Adelia? Are you all right?"

"Yes, sorry, I was just leaving."

"Already?" Renata asked. "We have plenty of time before we need to prepare."

"You know me. I like to be early."

"Let me come with you," Renata said, taking Adelia by the elbow. "We can run our lines together."

Adelia would have preferred a few minutes of complete quiet so she could think, but Renata looked so earnest. And really, more time stewing alone wasn't going to change her circumstances. She was still an actress and Fletcher was still a lord. And they still had a mission to complete.

"That sounds like an excellent idea."

"Give me a moment," Renata said, "I'm just going to let the others know that we're leaving. Did you want to wait for me in the foyer?"

"Yes, thank you, I'll meet you outside."

Adelia ducked out as Renata went to find their friends. Out in the foyer she could still make out the voices of those inside, but she couldn't hear what anyone was saying. She closed her eyes and focused on her breathing. Just like when she was anxious backstage, she could feel her heart rate calm, letting her think more clearly.

Obviously, Fletcher and his mother were at odds with respect to how he should carry on in the future. While the idea that he wasn't ready to follow the path his mother had set out should make her happy, Adelia couldn't help but think about what would happen to her if she ever were to accept Fletcher's proposal.

The tete-a-tetes with his mother would seem tame in comparison to what the rest of society would unleash on her.

The marriage proposal was a beautiful thought, but it wasn't something she could actually accept. Not to mention that Fletcher would regret the decision. That is assuming he didn't already.

Though, his actions throughout the day seemed to indicate that he still enjoyed her company, at least until the end when Meri's name had come up.

Thinking of Fletcher reminded her that she'd left him in the dining room without telling him where she was going. Adelia turned back when a familiar figure walked up to her. She smiled in greeting, but by the time she saw the white flowers, it was too late.

Fletcher looked foolish. He hated looking foolish.

Standing in the middle of a crowded dining room holding two plates, he'd been searching for Adelia for the past five minutes. He'd even gone outside, to the terrace, but there'd been no sign of her.

"You look lost."

Fletcher turned and saw a familiar looking young man standing at his elbow. It took him a minute to recall his name—Albert or Bertie. Yes, Bertie was what Adelia called him.

"I'm not, but I fear my escort is."

"Ah, yes. I'd been hoping to speak with Adelia myself but I think perhaps she must have left to prepare for tonight. I don't see Renata here either and that girl is Adelia's shadow."

Fletcher nodded his agreement but inside he was cursing. Damn Davis for taking up so much of his time. "Can I interest you in a plate?"

Bertie took the plate and patted his flat stomach. "I shouldn't really, but we're nearly at the end of the run."

"Will you be performing tonight as well?"

Bertie nodded, shoving a crab cake into his mouth. "I am, because Adelia asked, but really the crowd is there for her. The crowd is always there for her."

Fletcher chewed on a sandwich triangle. Despite his words, Fletcher didn't get the impression that Bertie was either jealous or lovelorn.

"And that doesn't bother you?" Fletcher asked, hoping he projected the usual calm, laissez-faire attitude he was known for.

"Bother me?" Bertie paused with a second crab cake halfway up to his lips. "You mean because Adelia is such a draw? I can see why you might think that, but I'm the one who discovered her. I begged her to audition for Mr. Davis. She was working in a—"

Bertie snapped his mouth shut.

"Where was she working?" Fletcher was both desperate to know, but at the same time told himself Adelia's past was irrelevant.

"I think that's Adelia's to tell."

Though he wanted to push, Fletcher knew the other man was correct.

"You're a good friend."

"The best." Bertie agreed. "Which is what Adelia deserves."

"I cannot argue with you there."

Their conversation came to an end as Bertie was called away by the reminder of his curtain call, leaving Fletcher to finish eating in solitude. He took out his pocket watch. The sun would be setting in a few minutes and it was almost time for him to make sure everyone was in place. If he left now he'd even have time to check on Adelia at the Assembly Hall. He knew she was more than capable of taking care of herself, but the fact that she'd left without telling him nagged. It wasn't like her.

Abandoning his plate on a nearby table, Fletcher nodded in the direction of Davis and some other men who would have stopped him for further conversation but he was on a mission. He headed out to the foyer and came to a halt when an all too familiar figure stepped in front of him.

Seeing his mother, Fletcher knew why Adelia had left so abruptly.

"What have you said to her now?"

"Only the things you should have said yourself. It's past time for you to settle down, and if you can't see that I had hoped perhaps the actress could be prevailed upon to step aside. It does your future bride a disservice to see you parading such a woman all over town."

"My future bride?" Fletcher could feel his temper rise and for once he didn't care if his mother saw him angry, didn't care that she would take his emotions and use them against him. "I think it would be wisest if you didn't continue talking about such a woman."

"Lady Fianna won't wait for you forever. Her mother confided in me that she has had no less than three offers this Season."

"Then perhaps she should accept one of them."

Lady Fletchingham adjusted her gloves. "That statement is beneath you. Lady Fianna is pretty, she has a good title and she's a favorite amongst the *ton*. We could hardly ask for better."

"Perhaps you could not ask for better, but I will insist upon it. I want a wife I enjoy spending time with, who enjoys spending time with me."

His mother waved a hand. "Husbands and wives don't need to spend time in each other's company."

"No, but it's what I want. I want a wife who has interests aside from planning dinners or looking over fashion plates."

"You're being unreasonable. All well-bred women enjoy running a house. It's a skill set you'll appreciate when you have a woman of breeding at your side."

"I'd prefer a woman of good character."

"Fortunately, you can have both."

"I'm glad you think so."

"Then we are on the same page. I'll speak to the Countess." Lady Fletchingham turned to walk away, evidently pleased with their conversation.

"Assuming you are speaking to her about returning to London to find a more suitable arrangement for her daughter, then by all means, go ahead."

His mother stopped, turning back to him with narrowed eyes. "I beg your pardon?"

"I won't be marrying Fianna or any of the other ladies you've picked out."

"And why is that?"

"I've already decided on a future wife. Now, if you'll excuse me, I'm going to go meet her."

Fletcher didn't wait for a response from his mother. He exited the inn, checking his watch in the dying light.

The conversation with his mother had set him back. Unfortunately there wasn't time to check on Adelia. Not, he reminded himself, that she needed it. She was more than capable of dealing with the fallout of a conversation with Lady Fletchingham while staying on task. It was one of the many things he loved about her.

Fletcher stopped walking, nearly tripping over his own feet.

Was he in love? It was such a foreign thought, but what

else could have compelled him to propose marriage?

He waited for a sense of dread to overtake him like a wave, but instead it was all calm seas. He loved Adelia.

But did she return the feeling? He began walking again.

Thinking about it, it seemed that Adelia liked spending time with him. Despite their awkward beginning, they'd come around to eating breakfast together every morning and had gradually gone from only discussing their mission to discussing themselves. Fletcher had been more open these past weeks with Adelia than he'd been with anyone else in...well, ever.

But had she been as open with him? Could she possibly feel the same?

"My lord?" Myles whispered into the night.

"It's me. Is everything set?"

"Yes, Sir."

"Excellent. Let's get to work."

CHAPTER TWENTY-THREE

"My source in London warned us that there are agents amongst us."

She looked around, taking in the simple drawing room with its wood panelled walls. Out the window she could see the ocean, though the view was partially obstructed by the gardens. Someone should cut those plants back. It was a shame to block such a view.

A frown started on Jackson's lips and rippled all the way up to his bald head.

"Any word on who the agents are?" She asked him.

"Unfortunately my source has not been privy to such information."

"Not even a description?"

"I'm afraid not. Though, they were quite certain that the agents would arrive with the acting troupe."

"I suppose that's where my expertise will come in. We'll need to be on the lookout for anyone with ties to the military."

"Would they be so obvious?" Jackson asked. "I think they'll send agents where we least expect it."

She tapped thick fingers against the mantle. "I've seen the manifesto. There's a lord travelling with the actors. The rumor *is that he's attached to an actress."*

"Surely you don't think an English lord would lower himself so?"

"No, but put a tail on his servants."

"I'll get right on it." Turning to leave, she caught sight of a reflection in the mirror over the mantle...

Adelia slowly blinked her eyes. It took a minute to adjust to the darkness. The smell of salt and damp filled her nostrils and she could just make out the cramped, chilly space she was in as the dying sunlight filtered in through cracks between planks of wood.

One thing she knew for certain, based on her last vision she needed to get to Fletcher. She'd been correct about Jackson, but they'd been all wrong about James Morrissey.

Forcing herself to a seated position, she waited for her head to settle so that the floor beneath her stopped moving. It took a minute to realize that the rocking wasn't in her head but all around her. She was on board a boat.

From the looks of it, she was in a holding cell. The light was too faint to make out more than shiplap walls and the outline of a barred window set in a door. Holding out her arms, Adelia could just touch the tips of her fingers off of the wood siding on either side.

Dropping her arms to her sides, she thought back to the last thing she could remember. She'd been at the inn. Fletcher's mother had cornered her again then she'd walked out into the foyer of the inn, only to turn around and find herself face to face with...

The door creaked open and light poured in. Once again it took some time for her eyes to adjust so that she could make out the figure in front of her.

"Renata? What's happening?"

The young woman stood in front of her, dressed in Adelia's costume for the evening. "You had us all fooled, didn't you?"

"Why are you wearing my dress?" Adelia's brain fought against the truth that was trying to force its way through.

"I deserve this," Renata said, "I've been waiting in the wings all this time while you've been stealing the spotlight and all along you've been hiding what you really are."

"What have I been hiding?" Adelia asked. She squinted in the lantern light. Her head felt like it had been squeezed in a vise.

"You're one of those girls with the fever," Renata hissed. "You've been unstable all this time."

Looking at Renata at that moment, with her wild eyes, Adelia didn't think that she was the one who looked unhinged.

"Let's talk this out," Adelia said, pulling herself to standing. Renata took a step back.

"Don't come near me!"

Adelia didn't want to hurt the girl, but she had enough training to know that she couldn't let herself be captured.

She was about to launch herself toward the hand holding the lantern, thinking it was the best to take away a possible weapon, when a man's voice called from down the hall.

"All right there, love?" Calen O'Donnell came around the corner and Adelia's heart sank as she noticed the pistol at his waist. How had she not seen it? It was Calen's perspective she'd been in during the visions. He'd been the one working with Jackson all along, not James. "We've got to go, it's almost time for your big debut. Don't worry about her. She'll be taken someplace where she can get proper care."

Renata hesitated in the doorway for a fraction of a second before turning away from Adelia and clicking the lock back in place. Adelia hurried to the window, but all she could see was the light from the lantern fading down the hall. She kicked the door and pain shot up her foot.

"Stupid," she muttered to herself as she leaned her head on the bars. Her heart raced and she knew that the first thing she needed to do was remain calm and develop a plan.

Taking a deep breath in through her nose and out her mouth, she thought back to the vision she'd had. She knew the two men talking had been Calen and Jackson. They hadn't known about herself or Fletcher, but they had said something about keeping an eye on the servants.

Myles.

If someone was watching Myles they'd realize their plan to intercept the girls.

She needed to warn them.

Taking a pin out of her hair, Adelia crouched down in front of the door, wishing she had a better source of light.

Fletcher took a seat near the back of the assembly

rooms. The recitations were already underway but he'd made it back sooner than expected. Myles had everything under control and the girls would easily be intercepted by their man at the docks and brought out to an airship instead of the rickety ship he'd seen in the harbor.

Settling into his row, he saw a thrilled looking Wilma seated near the front, her red curls lit up like flames in the light from the gas lamps. As Bertie finished giving an over-the-top yet entertaining rendition of the "to be or not to be" from Hamlet, Fletcher joined the rest of the audience in their enthusiastic applause and straightened in his seat, ready for the next performer.

Their diversion had worked so far. There were dozens of people coming through the town and while most were in the assembly rooms, the streets were filled with drivers and servants, meaning that not only did Fletcher and Myles not stand out, the routes through town that the ladies could take were greatly reduced, making it easier to keep an eye on their movements.

By the time Fletcher had left Myles, he'd already monitored the first group of women and had sent signals out to the airship, alerting the team that the women were on the way. Fletcher had waited to see the flashing light off shore, indicating that the message was received, before heading back to the assembly rooms to make sure his cover remained intact.

Borrowed gas lamps ringed the makeshift stage, lighting up on a figure in a green embroidered dress. It took Fletcher's brain a moment to process that the actress standing before them, speaking the lines to Ophelia's monologue wasn't Adelia.

He turned to the woman seated next to him, but she didn't appear at all surprised by the substitution. Had Adelia changed her mind about her recitation piece? Would she be out after?

"I expected Miss Dumont," Fletcher said, keeping his voice low enough so that only those around him would hear.

"You didn't hear?" The woman to his right gave a shake of her head. "She took ill right before the performance. Poor dear."

"Did she indeed?" Fletcher said as his insides turned to lead.

He got out of his seat as quietly as he could, knowing it was incredibly bad manners to get up in the middle of a performance but he couldn't wait. He needed to find Adelia and he needed to find her now.

He left the assembly hall and the cool night air hit his face. It did nothing to ease the sense of dread washing over him. He ran to the inn, taking the stairs up to their suite two at a time. He crashed through the door to find a startled Lilah sitting by the fire with a neat pile of mending at her side.

"My Lord." Lilah jumped to her feet. "What is the matter?"

"Is Adelia here?"

Lilah frowned. "Why would she be here? She has a performance."

"She isn't at the assembly hall. Someone is taking her place. They said she took ill."

Lilah dropped the lacy material she'd been holding. "That can't be true. She's never missed a performance."

"I know."

"I need to find her." Lilah looked around the drawing room as though a plan would appear in front of her. Her eyes were a little wild, a sure indication that she was starting to panic. It was a feeling Fletcher needed to push down. He stepped forward, taking the maid by her shoulders so that she focused on him.

"Take a deep breath," Fletcher ordered. He watched while Lilah's face relaxed into a calmer expression before releasing her shoulders and taking a step back. "What do you know of your mistress's work off-stage."

"Nothing specific."

"But you know she does some work on behalf of the Crown?"

"I suspected," Lilah nodded.

"I'm going to ask you to do something very difficult," Fletcher said.

"Anything."

"I need you to stay here and pretend everything is normal."

"But I want to help."

"It's of the utmost importance that no one suspect anything out of the ordinary. Should anyone come by, they need to think Adelia is settled away in that room."

"And you'll go find her?"

"I give you my word. I know it's hard not to act, but by staying here, by keeping her cover intact, you are performing a crucial task."

Lilah still didn't look convinced, but Fletcher had no time to waste. She gave him a quick nod and he left the suite, hurrying down the stairs and back out the inn.

The sun had fully set and it was difficult to see much of the view out over the water. Meri was somewhere out there. He hoped his friend had things under control on his end.

The sense of dread that had started as soon as Adelia had failed to appear on stage grew by the second. He should have kept a better eye on her, especially knowing Jackson suspected she had the fever. He'd been so stupid.

Fletcher headed toward Myles' lookout, hoping his valet had seen something that would give him a clue as to where Adelia had been taken. He slowed his pace as he approached the alcove overlooking the ocean. Fortunately there was just enough light from the rising moon to make out the shadow of a figure on the bench.

"Myles?" Fletcher whispered. "It's me. I need to know if you've seen anything strange."

As the figure on the bench turned to face him, Fletcher's stomach bottomed out.

"My lord," Jackson's face split into a grin. "How fortuitous we should meet again."

CHAPTER TWENTY-FOUR

Thank the heavens for rusty locks, Adelia thought to herself as she crept through the hallway outside her cell. She ran her hand along the wood paneling, both to guide her in the darkness and to keep her balance. She'd always been slow to get her sea legs.

She reached the end of the hallway, her foot hitting off what she hoped was a staircase to the upper deck. Adelia waited for a moment, listening for voices. All she heard was the lapping of the water against the side of the boat.

Hands stretched out, she clambered up the narrow staircase until fresh salt air hit her in the face. Her eyes adjusted to the moonlight and she could see enough to know that she was on the deck of a vessel. She couldn't be completely certain of the size, but based on the length of the hallway outside her cell, she didn't think it was overly large, more like a merchant vessel for local runs.

Moving slowly, just in case she wasn't alone, she made her way to the railing. Her heart sank as her eyes made out the lights on shore. She was much too far to swim.

She turned, looking to see if there was anything she could use as a raft, when she caught a flash coming from behind her. A light appeared for a moment, then vanished again.

Adelia rushed to the otherside of the deck, hoping for a better look. The light didn't reappear, but she thought she could make out the shadow of a ship.

"Of course," she whispered. "The airship."

She couldn't know for certain how close the other ship was parked, but based on where she'd seen the light, it was much nearer than the shore.

It was a risk. On the one hand she could aim for the shore and know that she was going in the direction of land even though there was a good chance she'd tire out before she came ashore. On the other, if the airship was indeed the shadow she'd seen, she was confident she could make it. But if her eyes were playing tricks on her, or if it was an unfriendly vessel, she could be in an even worse predicament.

She really was caught between the devil and the deep blue sea.

Closing her eyes, she took a deep calming breath.

There really was only one option.

Climbing over the railing, she mentally counted to three and jumped overboard.

The water closed around her, freezing her to the very core. Even when she pushed her way to the surface it took her several breaths before she could force her frozen lungs to work. She kicked off, heading toward the shadow ship.

Swimming in the ocean was nothing like the time she'd been in a country lake. Aside from the extreme cold, her skirts tangled in her legs, impeding her progress. She should have stripped down to pantaloons like she'd done on vacation. But the idea of showing up in front of strangers in nothing but wet undergarments wasn't appealing.

Not that showing up in front of strangers in a wet day dress was much better.

As she moved through the water, she tried not to think about the fact that she was moving further away from land. If she'd made a mistake, if the shadow she thought she saw turned out to be nothing, she wasn't sure she'd have the energy to even make it back to the boat she had jumped from.

Don't panic.

Focusing in on the task at hand, Adelia propelled herself forward, her limbs growing heavy. At one point she thought she saw another light, but she wasn't sure her eyes weren't playing tricks on her.

After what felt like ages but she knew was probably only minutes, the shadow rose before her. The clouds moved away from the moon long enough to show the outline of not only a schooner, but also a balloon.

If she had the energy to spare she would have cried with relief.

Treading water, she sized up the airship.

It wasn't particularly big—certainly not as big as the one she'd come to Belfast on—but it was tall enough that there was no way for her to reach the railing.

She knew there had to be a way up. The ship was here to collect the girls, therefore there had to be a way for them to get on deck. She swam along the side of the ship, her numb hands feeling for anything that might help her climb, when she brushed against a rope.

Not just a rope, a ladder.

Adelia grabbed on and tried to pull herself up, out of the water but her fingers fumbled and it took a few tries to hoist herself up. Between the cold and the weight of her wet clothes, it took most of her energy just to get out of the water. Her teeth chattered as she climbed and she nearly lost her balance reaching for the third rung.

When she was nearly halfway up, she heard voices on deck. They weren't clear enough to make out words, but she hoped they were close enough to hear her call out.

"Hello!" Adelia's voice was hoarse from the salt water. She took a deep breath and tried again. "Hello!"

She heard the sound of footsteps approaching, followed by a man's voice.

"Is someone down there?"

"Yes! And I need help."

Adelia felt the tug of the rope ladder, and she held on tighter, as she was pulled upward. She knew that once her fingers warmed up she'd have terrible rope burns, but at the moment she didn't care.

Once the railing was within reach, a pair of strong arms pulled Adelia the rest of the way over, holding her up when she would have fallen on the deck.

She looked up and even with only the light of the moon, she could see the glint of gold hair and brown eyes.

"Meri?"

"Adelia? Is that you?"

She threw her arms around his neck. "Thank goodness you're here. You have to help me save him."

Fletcher had been attacked from behind. He hated being attacked from behind. He'd come to in a dark room with the worst headache. There was no source of light, making it impossible to see anything. He could be in a closet or a ballroom.

Well, based on the smell he was fairly certain he wasn't in a ballroom.

"My lord? Are you awake?"

"Myles?" He sniffed again. Salt, something musty, old fish… "Are we on a boat?"

He tried to sit up, which is when he realized his hands were bound together behind his back.

There was a shuffling sound and Fletcher had an image of Myles shifting toward him.

"I wasn't conscious when I arrived," Myles said. "But based on the rocking I believe so."

"What's the last thing you remember?"

"Sitting at the lookout while the second delivery was brought to the airship. There was a third waiting on shore. I'm not sure if they made it or not."

Myles' voice held notes of dejection. It sounded so unlike his usual cheerful tone.

"No use worrying when we don't know. Better to focus on getting out of here. Wherever here is."

"I got a look around when they opened the door to throw you in. A man had a lantern and I saw the space was about five feet wide. I think it's a holding cell. I saw a similar one across the hall before the door closed."

"This must be the boat they were planning on using

to move the ladies." Fletcher leaned his head back against the wall. His headache dissipated just enough to make it easier to think more clearly.

"If it helps, I haven't heard any other voices down here."

"I'm not sure if that's a good thing or a bad thing. Adelia is missing."

Myles let out a rush of air. "Are you sure she's missing? Perhaps she went back to the inn."

"I spoke to Lilah."

"Well, if they kept us alive, there's no reason to think they'd harm her."

"No, I suppose not." Fletcher tested the ropes. The knots were too tight. There was no way he could free himself. "She's more valuable than we are."

"In what way?" Though he couldn't see Myles, Fletcher could still hear the curiosity in his voice.

"Can you keep a secret?"

"Don't I already?"

"This isn't my secret."

"Ah," Myles said, his tone turning serious. "It's about Miss Dumont then."

"It is."

"I swear to you to keep her secrets just as I keep yours."

Fletcher shifted and the ropes around his wrists chafed at the motion. He didn't like to spill details of Adelia's personal life, but in the event that Myles made it out and he didn't, it was essential for his valet to know how to protect her.

"She experiences the fever."

"Indeed? But she seems so very sound of mind."

"She is." Fletcher couldn't keep the bite out of his tone.

"Of course Sir, I didn't mean to indicate otherwise. I assume you have reason to believe that our hosts are also privy to this information?"

"I do."

"Well then," Myles said with some of his usual humor, "I suppose we ought to get out of here."

"I assume your hands are tied as well?" Fletcher asked.

"They are, behind my back. And yours?"

"Same. But if we can maneuver ourselves perhaps we can help each other."

"Yes, of course," Myles said. "Keep talking and I'll move toward you."

"Do you have any injuries?"

"A bump on the head. Nothing of note."

Fletcher could hear Myles shifting toward him and he did the same, pushing his shoulder blades together so that he could reach out behind him. At first his fingers flexed into dead air until he grasped onto what felt like a sleeve.

After a few minutes of fumbling, Fletcher got a hold to the ropes and was able to work the knots loose. As soon as he was freed, Myles started working on Fletcher's bindings.

"A bit of light wouldn't go astray," Myles muttered as he tugged on the ropes. Before he managed to get Fletcher loose, they were interrupted by the sound of footsteps coming down the hall.

"Sit down and act like your hands are still bound," Fletcher whispered.

"I already am," Myles said. "This isn't my first mission."

"Will all the girls fit in the cell with Miss Dumont?" A man asked. The voice had a lilt to it and sounded familiar. Fletcher had definitely heard it before.

"They don't need much space," another man spoke. There was no doubt in his mind who owned that voice. He'd recognize Jackson anywhere. "If necessary I'm sure the gentlemen next door won't mind the company."

Fletcher's heart felt ready to explode out of his chest. If Adelia was here, then she must be safe, at least physically.

The men continued toward them, their footsteps stopping and the sound of a cell door squeaking open filled the air.

"What's this?" The Irishman's voice came out as a growl. "This door isn't locked."

"What do you mean, the door is open?" There was a scuffling sound, presumably as Jackson moved in to see what was going on. "She's gone."

Fletcher froze. He didn't need clarification on who 'she' was.

"She can't have gone far. Search the ship."

"What if she's not here?" The Irishman asked.

"The only way out is overboard. If she took that route there's no point worrying about her now."

As the footsteps disappeared back down the hall, Fletcher held his arms out to Myles again. "Hurry. We need to get out of here and get to Adelia before they do."

"Yes, Sir." Myles got to work on the knots. Fletcher appreciated that the other man didn't ask what they would do if Adelia wasn't on board.

CHAPTER TWENTY-FIVE

Adelia paced back and forth as best she could in the cramped captain's quarters. She appreciated that Meri had set a roaring fire and had found her dry clothes, even if they were breeches.

But while she was immensely grateful, Meri seemed to be having a hard time understanding that they needed to get moving.

"Time is of the essence," she said for what felt like the hundredth time. But really, she couldn't have been on board more than half an hour. During that time Adelia had not only managed to get dry, she'd also learned that two dories had arrived with the ladies from the school and they were being well looked after in the living quarters below deck.

Unfortunately there was a third group of ladies that had been seen on shore but had yet to arrive.

"I want to make sure we have a solid plan before we move." Meri sat at a small desk, making notes. "We don't yet know for certain that anyone is in trouble."

"But we have to assume it," Adelia said, pausing in front of the fire with her hands out. The circulation had yet to fully return to her fingers. "Otherwise all the ladies would already be on board."

Meri frowned. "There's definitely something up. The fact that you were taken is evidence of that. What on earth could they have hoped to gain by kidnapping you?"

Adelia swallowed hard. Aside from Fletcher and her doctor, she'd yet to reveal her condition to anyone. But this was Meri.

"You know the reason these women have been abducted?" She asked him.

"I know they all suffer from the fever."

Adelia took a deep breath. "You know there are side effects? That some women have visions."

Meri laid down his pen, turning his attention completely to Adelia. "That information is classified."

"Not if you suffer from it," Adelia said, her voice dropping.

"You have the fever? Why have you never told me?"

"The same reason none of us tell anyone," a voice said from the doorway. Adelia turned to find Hazel standing there, watching her.

"I'm sorry, couldn't help overhearing," Hazel continued. "As soon as they told me you were on board I came right up."

Adelia stood frozen, searching for something to say when Hazel's words registered: *The same reason none of us tell anyone.*

"Not you too?" Adelia whispered.

Hazel walked across the small space until she was close enough to take Adelia's hands in her own. "It's why I insisted on coming tonight. No one can understand what these ladies have been through like I can."

Adelia could feel the warmth from Hazel's skin, reminding her of the reason she was on board.

"One of the visions I had, it involved Myles, Fletcher's assistant."

"And you think he's in trouble?"

Adelia nodded as she dropped Hazel's hands. "Jackson said something about following Myles. It wouldn't take much to realize Fletcher is connected."

"And with the final group of ladies still unaccounted for, perhaps we should be worried," Hazel finished. "What do you think, Meri?"

"I think I'm going to head back over to that boat Adelia came from to check things out. Hopefully this is all for nothing and while I'm gone the other ladies will show up along with a message from Fletcher."

"That's an excellent idea," Adelia said. She could finally feel the warmth seeping into her extremities. "How will we get there?"

"We?" Meri shook his head. "Not we. You're staying here."

"I'm not. I'm the one who knows the way around that boat."

"And I'm the one who can operate the dory," Meri said.

"Then you both go," Hazel said. "That's the reasonable solution."

"Is it?" Meri asked with a frown, but he didn't put up any further argument. Hazel gave her a quick hug before heading back below deck with the women.

"Duncan was not pleased about her coming on this

mission," Meri said when Hazel was out of earshot. "Especially since he couldn't come as well."

"Yet she's here," Adelia said as she followed him up to the deck.

Meri was all business, giving orders to anyone they passed—which wasn't very many people—and Adelia noted that no one was in military uniform. Not even Meri.

"Did you use leave time to come here?"

Meri glanced over his shoulder, a half smile on his face. "It's just two days. Besides, this is better than anything my mother would have had me doing."

Up on deck the night air was nippy. The fact that she'd been sitting in front of a fire probably made her more susceptible. It was also dark. The interior of the ship had been lit with gas lamps, but they couldn't risk it outside. Clouds were once again covering the face of the moon making it difficult for her eyes to adjust. Meri didn't seem to have the same problems as he had her hold onto the back of his jacket as they moved across the deck.

"All right," Meri said as they stopped at the railing. Adelia let go of his jacket and Meri took her hands and placed them on the rope ladder attached to the rail. "I'll go down first. Count to thirty before you follow because I want time to get oriented in the dory."

"How can you see?" Adelia leaned forward but everything was inky blackness.

"I've got my ways." She heard Meri climb over the railing. "Start counting."

Adelia started to count in her head. By the time she got to ten she listened for noises but she couldn't pick up on anything other than the lapping of waves. Once she thought she saw a glimpse of light, but it was so fast she wasn't sure if it was her eyes playing tricks on her. When she reached thirty she felt her way along the rail and held onto the ropes for dear life as she climbed down into the darkness.

She continued to count, not because she needed to, but because it took her mind off the darkness. She couldn't shake the feeling that she was slowly lowering herself into a void.

When she hit sixty-seven, her hands started to tingle from numbness. At eighty-three a hand lightly tapped her leg. Though it was just the barest touch, she was still startled.

"I'm going to guide you into the dory," Meri said.

Adelia felt strong hands on her waist as she descended into the boat.

"How on earth are you managing?" Adelia asked as the back of her legs bumped into a ledge. She crouched down, feeling a bench seat with her hands before lowering herself to sit.

"It's the training," Meri said, "I've had to spend a lot of time operating in shadows so getting around the deck was no trouble for me. For climbing down the ladder I had this."

Adelia saw a quick flash of something on the floor of the dory, but before she could get a good look it was gone again.

"What is that?"

"It's a portable aether light, a very small one. I can't leave it on for long, because I don't want anyone to see us, but it works in a pinch."

Adelia realized that must have been the flash she'd seen while standing on deck.

She heard the groan of wooden oars, then felt the dory jerk forward. She squinted, straining her eyes, but she could barely make out her own hands when she waved them in front of her face.

"I gather from your concern that you and Fletcher made out better as partners than previously anticipated?"

"Really? We're going to discuss this now?"

"I'm merely making an observation."

"Aren't you pleased? You wanted me to give him a chance."

For a few moments all Adelia could hear was the sound of the oars in the water. She wished she could see her friend's face, figure out what he was thinking about.

"I'm glad you're both getting along."

"I can hear the hesitation in your voice," Adelia said and heard Meri's sigh.

"Fletcher is a good man, but his mother has certain expectations."

"I'm aware."

"Indeed? And how did you gain that awareness."

"From Lady Fletchingham herself."

There was a scraping sound as though an oar had momentarily slipped. "You spoke to Fletcher's mother?"

"She spoke to me," Adelia said. "On more than one occasion."

"Do you mean she spoke to you in London?"

"No, Lady Fletchingham followed her son to Belfast.

You didn't know?"

"It's not like I've been hanging out in ballrooms," Meri said. "I wonder what compelled her to come all this way?"

"To marry her son off, of course."

"Or to prevent it," Meri said, his voice dropping. Adelia glared at him, but in the darkness it was a wasted effort. "I'll admit, when I saw how upset you were on deck I was worried. I know I told you to give Fletcher a chance, but I never intended for you two to form a serious attachment."

Adelia felt her face heat despite the cool air. "Why do you think that we have?"

"I know you, Del. I've never seen you so worried about anyone."

"We're friends, that's all. I don't need Lady Fletchingham's warnings to know a deeper relationship can't work."

"I wouldn't be so sure. Stranger things have happened."

"Stranger than a lord marrying an actress?"

"You've no idea." Meri's voice dropped, as though he was no longer speaking to Adelia. She was about to ask what he meant when the oars groaned to a stop and Meri held up the light. A single beam bounced off the hull of a boat not more than ten feet away.

"She's barely seaworthy," Meri muttered as the beam fell on a worn piece of siding.

"Do you see any way up?"

Meri ran the light along the side of the boat until it stopped on rope with heavy knots every few feet.

"You don't have to climb up," Meri said. "You can stay here and keep a lookout."

"Being a lookout is pointless and you know it. I can climb."

Adelia got out first and grabbed onto one of the knots. The rope was rough on her hands and she was grateful she'd changed into breeches as she pulled herself up.

The cloud moved just enough to allow a few rays of moonlight to peek through in time for her to see the top of the railing. She pulled herself over and moved out of the way for Meri to follow. He climbed the rope with ease, landing on the deck next to her like a cat.

"Where to?" He asked in a whisper.

"I was kept below deck," Adelia answered, matching his pitch.

"Lead the way."

The light from the moon made it possible for Adelia to maneuver her way around the deck but not to make out more than shadows. They crept along, listening for any sign of the men who'd kidnapped Adelia earlier. On the one hand, she appreciated that they didn't appear to be above deck, but did that mean they were down below? That would make it harder to investigate. She should have made Meri give her a weapon just in case.

Adelia was straining her eyes to see if there was anything around her that could be turned into a makeshift weapon when she felt Meri's hand grip her upper arm, holding her in place. It took her a few seconds, but then she heard it—the soft shuffling of feet.

Someone else was sneaking around.

Adelia cursed herself for not being more prepared

and was calculating where to hit a shadow for maximum results in a surprise attack, when it occurred to her that whoever these people were, they were also sneaking around.

Which meant they were likely allies.

Meri had the same realization as Adelia saw a flash of light hit the shadows in front of them.

"Who's there?" A familiar voice called. Adelia's lips tugged into a smile for the first time in hours.

"Myles?" She called. "Is Fletcher with you?"

Instead of an answer, Adelia saw a shadow moving towards her before she was swept off her feet into a familiar, slightly brandy scented, embrace.

"You're all right," Fletcher said, squeezing her against his chest. "I thought you'd jumped overboard."

"I did." Adelia's voice was muffled against Fletcher's chest. "That's how I found Meri."

Fletcher eased his hold enough for Adelia to take in a deep breath. Though she could sense that Fletcher was looking at her, she couldn't see much other than the flash of his eyes in the moonlight.

"Meri is here?"

The beam of light that had been trained on Myles shifted, lighting up Meri's face.

"Hello."

"You made it." Adelia could hear the relief in Fletcher's voice.

"Tell me you didn't doubt it?"

"I knew the ship had arrived, but I'd heard rumors that you might be tied up with something pressing."

Meri turned the light off, plunging them back into the shadows. "Nothing is more pressing than our work. Now tell me you know where the last group of women are."

Fletcher was grateful Meri had come. There were lots of decent pilots, but no one he trusted to the same extent.

Adelia fidgeted at his side but he refused to let her go. Though he couldn't see her in detail, nothing had ever looked as stunning to him as her outline in the moonlight.

"Our kidnappers took off a little while ago to intercept the last group of ladies. I don't think they know about the airship, but it's safe to say they have to be looking out for something."

"Then someone needs to get back there just in case," Meri said. "Hazel is on board with the other women."

"You didn't leave her alone?" Fletcher asked.

"No, but some warning for the agents on board wouldn't go astray. I'll double back. If you need a ride just point this toward the ship and I'll send someone over."

Meri held out his aether light.

"Don't you need it to see your way back?" Fletcher asked. On the one hand it would be an advantage to be able to see properly, but on the other he wouldn't leave Meri short.

"I have excellent eyesight. Don't worry about me."

"At least let me lead you back to your—how did you get here?"

"A dory, and why don't you let Myles accompany me. You look as though you need a minute."

It was in that moment Fletcher realized he was still holding Adelia firmly to his side. It wasn't that her presence was forgettable, on the contrary, it felt exactly like his arm was where it belonged.

"Allow me, my lord," Myles stepped forward and took the light, leading Meri back across the deck.

When they were out of earshot, Fletcher turned to face Adelia. The action was out of habit because he couldn't see her properly.

"Are you all right? I know you were kidnapped. I overheard the guards when I was brought on board."

He could feel Adelia shifting in his arms and he could swear she was trying to get a better look at him.

"I'm fine, but I was afraid I was going to be too late," she said.

"Too late for what?"

"Jackson suspected there was an agent travelling with the theater company. He wasn't working with James Morrissey, he was working with Calen O'Donnell."

"The actor?"

"Yes. They were tracking Myles and I was afraid you'd get caught too."

"How do you know they suspected Myles?"

"I had a vision."

"Of course." Fletcher pulled her against his chest and she stayed there. Perhaps it was the darkness that made her less hesitant. He didn't care.

"Are there any ladies on board? I wasn't able to take time to check the other cells before I escaped." Her voice was muffled where her cheek rested against his shirt.

"Not yet. Meri's men were able to intercept them. I think they'll try to bring the last group here before searching for the airship."

"Then what should we do to stop them?"

"Might I suggest we return the favor and knock them

out?" Myles' voice whispered from right behind them. Adelia flinched in surprise, but recovered quickly.

"How many are there?" She asked.

"There's Jackson and that must have been Calen we heard with him earlier. They've got to have someone running their dory as well. Our man would have been caught when we were."

"I hope he's all right," Adelia said.

"No reason to think he isn't," Fletcher said, squeezing her hip briefly. "Likely knocked out in a bush somewhere."

"So we need to be ready to take on three of them," Myles said.

"It'll be one for each of us then," Adelia said. "We should be able to manage that."

"Myles and I will manage," Fletcher corrected. "You'll keep a lookout."

Adelia pushed away and Fletcher was certain if he could see her face she'd be frowning at him.

"I've been trained for this, same as both of you."

"Not quite the same," Myles said, and Fletcher wished their faces were visible so his valet would know to be quiet.

"I'm not being the lookout," Adelia said, her voice firm.

"Fine," Fletcher agreed, though it was mainly because he didn't want her separated from him again. "But you'll stay at my side."

"Can you hear that?" Myles asked and the three of them went silent. Fletcher could hear the sound of oars hitting water.

"They're almost here. We need to get ready."

CHAPTER TWENTY-SIX

Adelia watched as Jackson held out a lantern for Calen as the younger man leaned over the railing. She hid in the shadows with Fletcher, waiting until the women were safely on board.

"I know it's more complicated this way," Fletcher had explained, "but it's important that the ladies are protected at all times."

While she waited, Adelia tightened her grip on the aether light. It was the shape of a candle, but instead of emitting a glow like a flame, it let out a beam of light. It also had a wind-up mechanism at the end, allowing it to be turned off and on.

Calen pulled on a rope until a woman's head appeared just above the railing. Adelia watched in fascination as the young lady was released from the makeshift harness. Though she was clearly conscious, it was evident from the way she allowed the men to maneuver her onto the deck that she wasn't completely present. Even when she was released, she stood still, not taking a step out of place.

When the third woman came into view Fletcher shifted slightly, as though trying for a better look. Adelia could see why when the light of the lantern momentarily caught the woman's face. She was an exact match to the likeness of Miss Mariah Cohen that she'd shown Captain Cartright.

As Adelia watched from their hiding place behind a barrel, the number of women increased until there were six on board. She was almost certain that was it for the ladies, but she waited until a ruddy faced man's head appeared above the railing. That would be the dory driver.

She felt Fletcher tap her upper back and sprung into action. Adelia stood up, blasting the aether light right into Jackson's face.

"Who's there?" Calen called, looking in Adelia's direction. Myles snuck up from behind, swinging a board of wood and knocking the actor out cold.

Jackson flailed his arms, trying to get free of the beam, but Adelia moved with him, keeping him blinded. At the same time the ruddy faced man headed toward Myles, which gave Fletcher an opportunity to come up from behind and take him out. Adelia smiled to herself as she watched Fletcher swing a board.

It was almost too easy.

She turned her attention back to her own task and noted that Jackson had managed to move toward her despite his temporary blindness. She backed up, coming up against the stack of barrels she'd been hiding behind.

"I'll get you," Jackson said, his fingers just inches from the hand holding the aether light. Adelia waited until he got closer, and kicked her leg out, making contact with his stomach and pushing him back where Fletcher was waiting to lay him out.

"Nice work," he said, squinting in her direction. Do you think you could lower your beam now?"

"Sorry." Adelia dropped the light. "Should I send a signal to Meri for some back-up?"

"I'll do it." Myles held out his hand. "Perhaps you want to check on the ladies?"

"Yes, thank you." Adelia handed over the light.

As she walked over to the group of women she noted that most took no notice of her, looking right through her as though she didn't exist. Such were the side effects of the *persephamine* drug. She picked up the overturned lantern Jackson had been holding, glad to see that while a pane had cracked, it hadn't broken. She stopped in front of Mariah, taking her cold hand in her own and was pleased when the young woman made eye contact with her.

"We're going to bring you home," Adelia said, giving the girl's fingers a squeeze. She got no reply.

"They'll recover," Fletcher said, stopping at her side. "And their families will help them through it."

"This could be me," Adelia said, releasing the girl's hand but keeping her eyes on the ladies. "It's only luck that I found Dr. Sahni."

"Much of our lives are luck," Fletcher said, resting a hand on her waist. "That's why we have to make the most of the things we can control."

As expected, Meri came to their aid with both a dory and several extra sets of hands to make the trek back and forth to the airship. Fletcher wasn't surprised when Adelia opted to wait until all the women were safely transported before agreeing to get into the dory herself. Once they were back on board, Adelia went below deck with Hazel to make sure all the women were taken care of. Fletcher followed Meri to the captain's quarters.

"Can I get you a brandy?" Meri offered as Fletcher took a seat near the fireplace.

"Make it a large one."

Meri chuckled as he went to a sidebar pouring a brandy and then a gin for himself.

"Cheers." Meri held out his glass and Fletcher tapped his own against it before taking a fortifying sip.

"What's your plan now?" Meri asked, taking the seat across from his friend. "Did you want to hitch a ride back to London?"

"It's tempting," Fletcher said. "But I think Adelia will want to close out her run."

Meri raised an eyebrow. "And you plan to accompany her?"

"Why wouldn't I?"

"Because your mission is technically over."

Fletcher paused with his drink halfway to his lips. When had he stopped thinking of his time with Adelia as being linked to their mission? He set his drink down on the table next to him.

"I asked her to marry me."

"Indeed? That is a surprise."

"She hasn't accepted."

"That's less of a surprise."

Fletcher eyed his friend as Meri finished the rest of his gin. He wondered if the rumors about Meri's own impending engagement were to be believed. His friend looked weary in a way that Fletcher had never seen before.

"Am I such a poor catch?" Fletcher's tone was light. Partly he hoped to draw Meri out, but he also wanted his friend's opinion.

"No, not you. But perhaps your mother is."

Fletcher picked up his glass, swirling the amber liquid. "Lady Fletchingham needs to mind her own business."

"But is she wrong? How would Adelia fit into your world? Can you really see her being content organizing dinner parties? Think about what you are asking Adelia to give up."

Fletcher frowned. "I haven't asked her to give anything up."

"Don't you have to?" Meri's mouth quirked in a smile that didn't reach his eyes. "Your future wife can hardly continue with a stage career."

"Why not?" Fletcher downed the rest of his drink. One of the things he enjoyed about Adelia was her independence. "It's not as though my lifestyle requires a full-time hostess."

In fact, it would suit him quite well to have a partner in life who had her own interests.

"You're serious?" Meri asked. "You think it's possible for Adelia to retain her own identity while marrying someone of your station?"

"I do."

Meri looked at him, tapping a finger against the arm of his chair. Fletcher wondered if his friend was thinking of Adelia's situation or his own.

"If that's how you feel, I think you should make your

expectations clear to Adelia."

"You think that would make a difference?"

"I think it might make all the difference."

Fletcher cleared his throat. "How about yourself? Is there anything you want to share about what has been keeping you so busy?"

Meri let out a harsh laugh. "My mission, such as it is, remains classified."

CHAPTER TWENTY-SEVEN

When Fletcher had decided against going back to London on the airship, Adelia had been surprised, though she couldn't deny that she was pleased.

Still, she reminded herself she had no reason to think his decision had anything to do with her.

Gossip was rampant in the little town of Briarwood, though no one really knew what had happened, they only knew the girls institute had abruptly shut down. The Agency's role remained a secret and the only persons who could have blown their cover were on their way to London in the cargo hold of an airship.

Lilah had Adelia's bags packed and ready to go. After throwing herself at Adelia as soon as she'd stepped into the suite, the maid had gotten herself firmly under control and arranged for a hot bath. She'd also suggested a nap while she got the trunks together, but Adelia had been too jittery from the events of the night before to sleep.

Besides, she could sleep in the carriage.

"I think it would be wiser for you to spend today resting," Lilah muttered as she did one last sweep of the suite to ensure there was nothing left behind.

"I have a performance tonight," Adelia said. "An important one."

They were already short one actor with the mysterious disappearance of Calen O'Donnell. Having no idea that his lead actor was on his way to stand trial in Britain, Mr. Davis had ranted about foreign talent and told Marco Lister, the understudy, to prepare to go on stage. Adelia had tried not to laugh as Marco lost his usual blustering attitude and immediately set about remembering his lines.

Her own understudy had also disappeared, though Fletcher had said he'd assign an agent to be on the lookout for her.

"Still, I think you should consider your health," Lilah said, not ready to drop the subject.

"I have, and I feel fine," Adelia assured her. "Now, if it's all the same with you, I'm going to go downstairs to wait for the carriage."

Adelia ran into Myles in the hallway, heading toward her suite. He gave her a quick nod and she noted that he looked none the worse for wear from their nighttime adventure.

"Good morning, Miss, you are looking well this morning."

"I very much doubt it, but it's kind of you to say so."

Myles grinned. "I was about to check in with your maid about our carriage back to the city, if that's all right?"

"Of course. She's in the sitting room."

Myles nodded again and headed into the suite. Adelia watched the door close behind them and was ever so briefly tempted to listen in on their conversation. She wondered if her suspicions about the two of them were correct, but she knew it wasn't fair to invade her maid's privacy. She'd have to wait until Lilah chose to reveal the relationship herself.

As her foot hit the stairs her stomach rumbled and she was reminded of the fact that aside from some biscuits Meri had forced on her the night before, she couldn't recall the last time she'd properly eaten. Seeing the grandfather clock in the foyer, she thought she might just have time to visit the dining room before they were due to leave for Belfast.

She was walking across the foyer when she heard the sound of her own name coming from the courtyard outside. Adelia looked around to see who was calling for her when she saw the open window and realized that what she'd overheard was someone's conversation. Her mood dropped as she realized that the individuals speaking were Fletcher and his mother.

Was she never to be rid of Lady Fletchingham?

Normally she would have moved on, giving them privacy much like she'd done with Lilah and Myles, but as they appeared to be discussing her, she made an exception and moved closer to the window.

"Surely you must see that you are wasting your time?" Lady Fletchingham said. "Parading about with this actress when you should be settling down with a wife."

Adelia couldn't see Fletcher's expressions, he was mostly in profile, but the way they were positioned gave her a clear view of Lady Fletchingham's face.

"I will agree that I need a wife," Fletcher said.

Lady Fletchingham's face visibly relaxed while Adelia's stomach twisted into knots.

"Then this is the last word we will exchange on the matter of Miss Dumont," Lady Fletchingham said.

"Indeed," Fletcher agreed. "It is."

The sound of footsteps drew Adelia back to the present and reminded her she was basically standing in the middle of a public foyer, eavesdropping on a conversation between two peers.

She turned to find Bertie coming down the stairs.

"You're still here," Adelia said, relief flooding her.

"I'm taking a carriage just after breakfast," Bertie said.

"Do you think there's room for one more?"

"Aren't you traveling with Lord Fletcher and Mr. Davis?"

Adelia couldn't tell the truth; that she was avoiding Fletcher because she knew their time together was coming to an end and she wasn't confident she could properly control her emotions.

"I'd like to get back to the city early," Adelia said, and it was the truth. "It will give me more time to prepare for tonight."

She could tell Bertie didn't quite believe her, but rather than ask questions, he gave her a soft, sad smile.

"You know I'll never turn down your company. You go ahead and get some breakfast and I'll make the arrangements."

Adelia leaned in and gave Bertie a quick peck on the cheek and then hurried into the dining room, hoping she'd managed to hide the tears filling her eyes.

She should have paid better attention to her own visions. It wasn't as though she hadn't been warned about Lord Fletcher.

I could never care for someone like you.

Adelia had left without him.

Fletcher stood in the courtyard as Davis delivered the message.

"She said something about wanting to get back to town early," Davis said. "You know how flighty actresses can be."

Fletcher knew no such thing, but he didn't want to get drawn into an unnecessary discussion with Davis so he climbed into the carriage and settled in for a tedious ride back to Belfast.

At least he had been successful in sending his mother back without him. He had no doubt that she'd continue interfering in his life, or at least attempting to, but once he'd made his intentions towards Adelia as clear as he possibly could, she'd walked off in a huff.

After running into his mother, and the unfortunate conversation that had ensued, Fletcher had been looking forward to a conversation with Adelia, though he knew they couldn't talk about anything meaningful while Davis was travelling with him, which was why he was able to keep his disappointment in check.

"I assume you'll be attending tonight's show?" Davis said. "Given that it's our closing night."

"I wouldn't miss it," Fletcher said.

"You'll be pleased to hear that I've secured the Prime Minister's box. I expected the Morrisseys would want it, but I received word they would not be in attendance to-night."

Fletcher still wasn't convinced the Morrisseys, and James in particular, weren't a little guilty of something, but they would have to be followed up on later, as would the whereabouts of the ladies who'd already been sent back to England over the last few months, as per Captain Cartright's reports.

"I'm glad you'll have such an excellent view, but I'm hoping to secure better seats."

Davis frowned, eyebrows coming together like the wings of a gull. "What seats could possibly be better."

"The floor."

"The floor?" Davis repeated. "You can't be serious."

"Of course I am."

Fletcher fought off the urge to laugh at Davis' confused sputtering. He was feeling so much better than he had in days.

When they arrived back in Belfast, Fletcher was disappointed—though not surprised—to discover that Adelia was already at the theater.

"She usually likes to take some extra time on closing night," Lilah explained. She and Myles had been given tickets to the show that evening and both were bustling about all afternoon getting trunks packed for the return to England the next day.

Feeling like he was only in the way in the suite, Fletcher decided to dine out for supper. He went to a nearby pub, attempting to blend in with the locals before heading to the theater to line up for tickets.

If Lady Fletchingham could have seen him, lined up

outside, waiting for entry like a common chimney sweep, she likely would have fainted from embarrassment. The thought brought a chuckle to his lips and caused more than one patron to look in his direction. Fletcher gave a brief nod and was careful not to draw any further attention to himself as the line continued to move.

Once in the theater Fletcher went to a seat only three rows back. He knew the actors could see the first row, but he thought he'd be able to blend in while still having an excellent view. As the lights dimmed, the crowd seated around him wasn't completely quiet, not like when he was seated in one of the boxes, but as soon as the actors came out in the opening shipwreck scene, the murmuring stopped.

Even though he'd already seen the show, Fletcher couldn't help but be swept along, especially when Adelia came out on stage for the first time.

CHAPTER TWENTY-EIGHT

It wasn't possible.

As Adelia delivered her opening lines she caught sight of Fletcher in the audience. She didn't let her gaze linger, but as she continued the scene she could feel his eyes on her. She exited the stage, hurrying away from her usual waiting area with the other actors, needing a moment to compose herself.

Why wasn't he sitting in one of the boxes? Why was he even here at all? They needed to start putting some distance between themselves publicly so that when they returned to London he could propose to the countess' daughter.

She drank a glass of water and took some deep breaths. Likely this was his way of saying good-bye. Fletcher had never gotten to do common things like sit in an audience and he surely wouldn't once he was properly married. This was his last chance.

Adelia's heart twisted thinking of Fletcher living the boring life of a lord. He was so much more. At that thought she laughed to herself. She was being foolish. This was the world Fletcher had been raised in. He was probably looking forward to putting aside his duties with the Agency and settling down.

Returning to the stage, Adelia finished the show, careful not to let her gaze linger for any length of time in Fletcher's direction. At least, she didn't until the curtain went down and she came out to take a bow. At that time she looked towards the third row and found an empty seat. Her heart sank but she kept the smile on her face as she took a second bow.

"You were fantastic!" Bertie said as she exited the stage. "One of your best shows."

"Thank you," Adelia said, turning to head toward her dressing room. Beulah stepped forward to walk with her and it occurred to Adelia that what she needed most was a moment to herself. "Would you mind giving me a few minutes before you come to my dressing room?"

"Of course," she said. "I'll go collect the other costumes first."

Adelia could feel the tears pricking at her eyes but she took a deep breath through her nose and got herself under control. Fletcher leaving like this was easier. In all likelihood he'd returned to the hotel and would already be in his rooms for the night when she arrived. With their early departure the following morning, it was entirely likely they wouldn't spend any further time alone in each other's company.

Which was for the best.

Adelia opened her dressing room door and was so grateful for the opportunity to have a moment to herself, that at first she didn't realize she wasn't alone.

Fletcher had decided to duck out of his seat right before curtain call. The fact that everyone in the cast and crew had seen him spending time with Adelia for the last fortnight meant that he could move around backstage with no one stopping him. The look of surprise on her face as she opened the door made missing the final curtain call completely worth it.

"You're here." For a moment she just stood in the doorway, but then she seemed to get her bearings and entered the small room, closing the door behind her. Fletcher fought the urge to take a step toward her, but they needed to talk first.

"Do you mind? I wanted to speak to you but it can wait if you want to change first."

Adelia took the seat in front of her dressing table, and Fletcher sat across from her on the settee. He noted that her posture was very straight and her face was slightly pinched as though she was suffering a headache.

"No, it's fine, we should talk."

"Are you sure? You seem unwell."

Adelia looked at a spot over his shoulder. "I'd really rather get this conversation over with."

"Over with?" Fletcher frowned. "That's how you feel about talking to me?"

"How do you expect me to feel when you've come here to cut our connection."

"Cut our connection?" Fletcher knew he sounded ridiculous repeating her words and gave himself a mental shake. "Is that what you want?"

There was a spark in her eyes when she turned her

attention to him. "I assume this is what you want. I over-heard you talking to Lady Fletchingham this morning be-fore we left Briarwood."

"Indeed?" Fletcher should have known his mother was at the root of this." And what exactly did you hear?"

"You were agreeing with your mother that you need-ed a wife and then Lady Fletchingham commented that this would be your last exchange about Miss Dumont and you agreed."

"And what else did you hear?"

"That was all."

"That's it? Nothing else?"

Adelia threw her hand up. "What else did I need to hear?"

"Perhaps the part where I explained to my mother that I had already asked you to become my wife, there-fore it would be improper for her to refer to you as Miss Dumont."

Adelia stilled. "You didn't."

"Of course I did."

"But...she must be furious."

Fletcher couldn't help the grin that broke out on his face. "Oh yes."

Adelia struggled to find words. Fletcher had never seen her sputter before and he had to force himself to keep a straight face. "You must have told her you never meant the proposal."

"I did no such thing. I told her that if she wanted to continue to be a part of my life she could accept my de-cisions. Otherwise she could move to one of the country estates."

Adelia leaned back in her chair looking both dazed and deflated. "I thought you came here to end things."

"I came here to get an answer. I asked you to marry me and you never responded."

"It could never work. People will never forget that I was an actress."

"Of course not, particularly since I'd never want you to give it up."

A bubble of hysterical laughter escaped Adelia's lips. "You can't be serious?"

"I'm not here to ask you to give up your life, I'm here to ask you to spend it with me."

"But you're a lord."

"I hadn't forgotten."

"And I'm an actress."

"I had noticed."

Adelia took a deep breath, her brows pinching together. "I need to tell you something."

"Why do I think I won't like this?"

She looked at him, meeting his gaze. "You remember the night we went to the Bombay Spectacle? You introduced me to Miss Lovejoy."

Fletcher thought back. It was only a few weeks ago, but it felt like ages. "Yes, she's an incredible gossip. I thought I'd explained that?"

"That's not what's important." Adelia fidgeted with the pleats of her skirt. "What I didn't tell you was that I had a vision that night."

Fletcher remembered thinking she was unwell for a moment. "I'm sorry, I didn't realize what was happening."

"I was fine, really. I didn't realize how the visions worked at the time but I realized soon after that the vision I had was from Miss Lovejoy's perspective."

Fletcher snorted. "I can only imagine what you were subjected to."

"Actually, you probably can. You were in the vision."

He wasn't certain how long it lasted, but Fletcher's whole body had gone perfectly still. Like he was trapped in a statue of himself. "What did you see?"

Adelia pulled at her skirt. Her eyes were filled with sadness. "I saw the end of your affair. I heard you tell her you could never care for someone like her."

"And you would hold it against me?"

"I suppose you can't help it. You weren't raised to care about people from the lower classes, people like me."

"Class has nothing to do with it." Fletcher stood up, the immediate effects of his shock at being a part of one of Adelia's visions wearing off. "Ronnie is a conniving woman who tried to blackmail me into continuing our relationship. I'm not proud of how I spoke to her, but I don't think I should be judged on that one interaction."

"You didn't end things because of where she came from?"

"Hardly," Fletcher said. "I barely began things because I quickly learned what kind of woman she was."

Adelia blinked. Twice. "I...I hadn't realized."

"Could we get back to the proposal at hand?"

"You actually want to marry me?"

"I wouldn't keep asking if I didn't."

"You don't even know my real name. Adelia Dumont is a stage name."

Fletcher sat back down. "Does anyone call you by anything else?"

Adelia shook her head.

"Then I think we're fine. It's not like I was born Lord Fletchingham."

Her face lit up in a slow smile. "Do you really think we could make this work?"

Fletcher leaned forward and took Adelia's hands in his own. "Do you think it's worth trying?"

She looked from their clasped hands and back up to his face before finally answering. "Yes, I think we're worth it."

CHAPTER TWENTY-NINE

"The ring is beautiful." Hazel leaned over Adelia's hand to get a better look at the square cut ruby. "Fletcher did an excellent job."

The two women were sitting in the drawing room of Adelia's flat with a small gathering of their closest friends. Fletcher had suggested they have a proper engagement ball, but Adelia hadn't wanted to give the *ton* an opportunity to snub her so openly. At least, not yet. Lady Fletchingham had already made her distaste more than clear and Adelia knew that was a battle that would continue for some time.

"He truly did." Adelia glanced across the room to where Fletcher stood in conversation with Meri and Duncan. As though he could feel her gaze, he turned toward her and raised his still full brandy glass in a salute.

"I'm so pleased that you aren't giving up your career," Hazel said. "The theater isn't ready to lose you."

"Just as the newspaper wasn't ready to lose you?"

Hazel took a sip from her champagne glass. "And why should either of us give anything up? Our future husbands won't have to."

"Speaking of, how are plans going for your wedding?"

Hazel scrunched her nose. "You'd have to ask my mother. I'm afraid I haven't been particularly involved. If it were up to me, Duncan and I would wed by special license. Or perhaps eloped to Scotland."

"That's likely what Fletcher and I will do. Neither of us wants a big ceremony and his mother certainly doesn't want to step in to plan one."

"I think that's charming," Hazel said. "I'm a little jealous."

There was laughter across the room and Adelia looked over again to see that Fletcher and Duncan were sharing a joke, but while Meri was smiling, his eyes appeared troubled.

"Have you heard the rumors about Meri's mission?" Adelia asked in a low whisper.

"Nothing official," Hazel said, leaning in so their heads were nearly touching. "Only that it has to do with the princess."

"Not really?" Adelia knew she was doing a terrible job hiding her surprise. "They met once before, you know."

Hazel frowned. "Duncan mentioned it, but he was sketchy on the details. If the rumors are true, I hope she makes him happy."

Adelia clinked her glass off of Hazel's. "You and I both."

"What do you suppose they're talking about?" Duncan nodded toward the settee where Adelia and Hazel were in a tete-a-tete.

"Whatever it is, looks to have their complete attention," Fletcher said, sipping his brandy. "So it obviously can't be us."

Meri glanced at his pocket watch, something Fletcher had almost never seen his friend do before. At least, not while on land. "I have to be going, I'm due at the opera this evening."

"Glad you could come celebrate," Fletcher said. "I know it meant a lot to Adelia."

"I'd never let her down," Meri said. "You either. I hope you're both very happy."

Meri said his good-byes to the ladies and Hazel and Duncan took their leave soon after. Fletcher settled on the settee with Adelia, finishing his brandy.

"This evening was nice," Adelia said, picking up a novel she'd started that afternoon.

"You're sure you don't want something more lavish to announce our engagement?"

Adelia laughed. "I perform in front of hundreds of people each evening for my living. I don't want or need large gatherings in my personal life."

Fletcher smiled as she opened her book but instead of reading, she turned back to him.

"Do you think Meri is all right?"

Fletcher frowned. "Should I be jealous of how much concern you show my friend?"

"He's my friend too," Adelia said with a dismissive wave. "And I'm allowed to worry about my friends."

"Indeed, but in this case, I think things will work out."

"You really think so?"

Fletcher nodded. "He may be uncertain now, but I think he'll find happiness in the end."

"But a princess? It seems so...un-Meri like."

Fletcher leaned forward and plucked the book off Adelia's lap, tossing it to one side.

"What are you doing?" She yelped.

"Trying to get my future wife's attention."

A smile pulled at the corners of Adelia's lips. "You have it. Now what are you going to do with it?"

Fletcher leaned forward, taking both her hands in his. "I'm so glad you asked."

Acknowledgements

I am very grateful to Lauralana Dunne for once again beta reading this work at various stages and giving wonderfully constructive feedback. Also thanks to my editor on this project AJ Ryan for being much more careful with names and commas than I ever could be.

Thanks to Matthew LeDrew for layout and technical support and to Ellen Curtis for cover design.

As always I'd like to think my awesome husband Mike for being my last line of defense copy editor and generally supportive partner.

Also from Amanda Labonté

HEED THE CALL

After a heated fight at sea between twins Ben and Alex, Ben vanishes from their boat without a sound or even a ripple in the water. Unwavering in his dedication to find his brother, Alex begins the adventure of a lifetime armed only with the help of a local girl named Meg and his own mysterious musical abilities... the key to which, and to the mysteries that surround him, may be tied to the alluring song of the dangerous girl he finds among the ocean's frothing waves.

#1 OCCULT BESTSELLER!

College freshmen Liesel Andrews spends her days studying pre-med and her nights stitching up werewolf bites.

Buy the book that Ali House raves "gives the pre-existing mythology of vampires some new blood!"

Photo by Joy K. Gallant

ABOUT THE AUTHOR

Amanda Labonté is a international bestselling author living in St. John's, Newfoundland, where she gets much of the inspiration for the characters and places about which she writes. Though she knew she wanted to be a writer since the eighth grade, it was many years before she finally walked into a creative writing class and found a new home.

Amanda is the co-owner of an educational business and a mother of two, and as such she spends much of her day with kids of all ages. They give her some of the best reading recommendations.

She has written seven novels: *Call of the Sea, Drawn to the Tides, Return to the Depths, Supernatural Causes* Volumes 1 & 2, *Lady of Vision,* and, *Mistress of Insight,* all of which are available through Engen Books.